VP

TH G.M.

Lo 7

E

DATE DUE		
8-01	Dockery	
9-01	W Ikmphy	
12-02	SH	
10-2-03	K Lile	
	E. Bliff	
8-04	Arnold	
7-05	A.J.	
10-06	WRC	
8	RY	
GAYLORD		PRINTED IN U.S.A.

THE SHERIFF
OF SALT CREEK

Sheriff Thomas Cavendish returns to Salt Creek little suspecting that his peaceful existence is soon to be shattered. The new man in town, Irwin Kaye, does his damnesdest to rid himself of Salt Creek's lawman. Meanwhile, Cavendish is trying to save a pretty female outlaw from the hangman's noose, but he finds the town turning against him. He stands firm, but falls foul of a dangerous adversary and knows he must use all his wiles to save himself.

M. DUGGAN

THE SHERIFF OF SALT CREEK

Complete and Unabridged

LTW
CC 6/01
14.⁹⁹
0989

LINFORD
Leicester

First published in Great Britain in 2000 by
Robert Hale Limited
London

First Linford Edition
published 2001
by arrangement with
Robert Hale Limited
London

The moral right of the author has been asserted

British Library CIP Data

Duggan, M.
  The sheriff of Salt Creek.—Large print ed.—
Linford western library
  1. Western stories
  2. Large type books
  I. Title
  823.9'14 [F]

  ISBN 0–7089–4543–0

Published by
F. A. Thorpe (Publishing)
Anstey, Leicestershire

Set by Words & Graphics Ltd.
Anstey, Leicestershire
Printed and bound in Great Britain by
T. J. International Ltd., Padstow, Cornwall

This book is printed on acid-free paper

1

Sheriff Thomas Cavendish slumped wearily against his saddle. The ride home had been long, and the day, in his opinion, was hotter than hell. The arm-pits of his plaid shirt were soaked with sweat; sweat trickled between his shoulder blades and down his belly, and all he could think of right now was a long soak. Never had the sight of the Salt Creek bathhouse been so welcoming. He needed to relax in a hot tub and to scrape the stubble from his face whilst his dust-coated duds were laundered. He needed a lot of things!

What he did not need was to see old Bart Parker heading his way. The old man had been seated, as always, before the general store, Perkins Emporium, but when he had spotted the sheriff Bart had hauled himself out of his rocker and now, with alacrity, making

1

good use of his stick, he was heading towards him.

To Thomas Cavendish, as he had ridden into town, the place had looked pretty much as it always had. Kids played, women shopped, old-timers snoozed on the sidewalks and the wooden Indian still stood outside the barber's shop.

'Hold on there, Sheriff,' Bart cackled, seemingly oblivious to the scowl which now marred Thomas's normally affable features.

'Howdy, Bart,' Thomas muttered reluctantly. 'I'm in kind of a hurry and — '

'Finished your business in Garland, have you?' the oldster interrupted with undisguised curiosity.

'Yep.' Thomas did not feel inclined to elaborate. Word would reach Salt Creek soon enough as to what its sheriff had been up to in Garland. Thomas did not feel a need to satisfy Bart's curiosity.

'You've been gone some time,' the oldster ruminated.

'Yep.'

'I heard you were helping Sheriff Duffy,' Bart essayed.

'You heard right,' Thomas replied wearily. Bart could gab for hours if given the chance.

'Didn't know you two were acquainted.' Bart was openly fishing.

'We go back a long way. Duffy and I grew up together. Now is that all? I need a bath. I'm beginning to stink like a polecat and I ain't inclined to waste my time with idle chatter just to suit you, Bart.'

Cavendish's eyes scanned the side-walks. Nobody that he could see showed the slightest interest in the fact their lawman had returned. It occurred to him that the people in this town paid him as much attention as they paid the wooden Indian. This observation did not unduly disturb Cavendish; he had never been one to throw his weight around.

Salt Creek had always been a sleepy little town. Cavendish was the town's first sheriff. There had not, he recalled, been competition for the job. No one else had been interested. This was not surprising, for the stipend could only be described as lousy.

Cavendish had a hunch that if anyone else had applied he would not have been given the job. He had to admit he was not a sight to strike fear into anyone's heart. They had even asked if he could use a .45!

'I'm wearing one, ain't I?' he'd replied testily.

'Well, we don't expect you'll be called on to use your Peacemaker much here,' had been the laconic reply.

'Well that suits me just fine,' he had replied. 'I'm a peaceable man who does not look for trouble.'

They had laughed at that and had managed to make him feel slighted, their laughter implying he was afraid of trouble.

He'd nodded and held his tongue for he had a widowed sister and numerous nieces dependent upon him to find them a place.

'Good. Draw up the contract!'

His sister, Ivy Tucker, would do as well in Salt Creek as anywhere. 'I've responsibilities,' he had admitted.

No one had enquired what his responsibilities were. He guessed no one gave a damn!

He'd been settled in Salt Creek for six months before anyone discovered the large woman who'd moved in with him was in fact his stepsister and the girls were his nieces.

'Well, that explains it, them being stepbrother and sister,' the minister's wife had exclaimed loudly, unaware that he was within earshot. 'A woman that size wouldn't naturally have a brother as short as — ' She'd shut up quickly for her companion having spotted the sheriff had nudged her.

'There's something you ought to know, Sheriff.' There was a sly look in Bart's watery eye which implied Cavendish would not like to know at all!

'And you're going to tell me. Well,

spit it out. I ain't got all day.'

'There's a new man in town.' Bart paused expectantly but Cavendish remained silent knowing that eventually Bart would get to the point. 'Irwin Kaye is his handle,' Bart divulged, clearly disappointed with the sheriff's lack of interest. 'Irwin's bought old Brocklehurst's spread.'

Thomas nodded. Old Brocklehurst had died recently. A stroke, Doc said.

Bart spat. 'He's a big shot. I've seen his kind before. I ain't always hung my hat in Salt Creek.'

'And?' Cavendish was not particularly interested where Bart might have hung his hat.

'And Irwin Kaye's boy has blasted a drifter.' Bart spluttered, finally reaching the point.

'Dead?'

'Planted six feet under,' Bart confirmed. 'Town buried him in an unmarked grave. If anyone looks for him they won't find him. It was murder, Sheriff, although no one will come out and accuse Patrick Kaye.'

'Murder?' Cavendish queried.

'Certainly. The drifter seemed not to know one end of a .45 from the other.'

'That bad,' Cavendish muttered. 'Then it wasn't a fair fight,' he mused, knowing there was not much he could do except watch the two Kayes.

'Depends how you see it, Sheriff. Fact is, the drifter was a farm boy. Like I told you he hardly knew one end of a Peacemaker from the other. Patrick Kaye provoked the fight. It was his way of testing himself. I'd say it was first blood, his first killing. He seemed mighty pleased with himself. So what are you gonna do, Sheriff?' Bart demanded.

'I'm gonna have my bath.'

'Hell, you're the kind of lawman this town deserves! Next thing I know Kaye will have you on private retainer. Either that or he'll scare the — ' Bart was forced to finish his tirade as Cavendish, ignoring him, dismounted, handed Bart the reins, stepped around him and

7

headed into the bathhouse.

Well, hell, Cavendish reflected, as he sank gratefully back in his hot tub, Irwin Kaye sounded as though he had the makings of another Colonel Parker.

Cavendish had just assisted his friend Duffy in taking care of the colonel and his sons, as well as a few of the colonel's crew.

After the colonel's death, the rest of his men had suddenly seen sense. They were tangling with the law after all. Duffy, as Garland's lawman, had arrived to arrest the colonel for the lynching of a young dirtbuster.

'I ain't got a choice,' Duffy had griped. 'One of the colonel's boys blasted the farmer's wife. In error, he says, but . . . ' Duffy had shrugged. 'The colonel's pushed me too far. This time I can't turn a blind eye to his wrongdoing.'

Duffy and the colonel had been friends. They'd fought together; the colonel had in fact been Duffy's commanding officer.

The colonel's mistake had been to count on old loyalties and to disregard completely the fact that Duffy was now sheriff when he was intent upon breaking the law.

At the last moment Duffy hesitated. It was Cavendish who fired the shot which shattered the colonel's head.

Cavendish sank back in the soapy water. If Irwin Kaye thought Salt Creek's lawman would turn a blind eye whilst his son committed murder, Kaye was mistaken. Salt Creek might pay a miserly wage, but even so Cavendish would uphold the law without fear or favour.

He closed his eyes. His imagination ran riot. He could just hear the folk of Salt Creek discussing him with Irwin Kaye. You won't need to worry about Sheriff Cavendish, he's a no-account little runt.

Way back, an unfortunate *hombre* had described Clem Cavendish's stepson as a miserable little runt. That *hombre* had no idea how near death he was, for Clem Cavendish, Thomas's stepfather, had taken the insult personally. Afterwards, Clem Cavendish, together with Thomas and his own daughter Ivy, had enjoyed a hearty meal.

'You just can't let insults get you down, Tom. Tuck in and enjoy yourself,' Clem had advised.

Thomas and Ivy had eaten until they couldn't manage another mouthful. Thomas smiled fondly as he remembered Clem. There was no doubt in his mind that he owed Clem Cavendish a debt of gratitude. Thomas had shown little aptitude for the Peacemaker, but Clem had persisted, maintaining Tom had no choice other than master the Colt .45.

'Ain't no other way you can defend yourself,' Clem had advised sadly. 'You've just got to blast them before they land that first blow, or put that first boot in. It's my duty to learn you and I ain't quitting.' Day in, day out, Clem had tutored Thomas until eventually Clem had pronounced he would do nicely.

Thomas had never hankered to be a gunman, or even a lawman; he'd taken the job of sheriff because he'd needed a place for Ivy, who was in dire straights at the time. The bank had repossessed the Tuckers' farm due to Hiram's mismanagement, his gambling and drinking, and then, to cap it all, the drunken Hiram Tucker had drowned in a bathtub.

No one had been surprised. Hiram had headed home that night as drunk as a skunk and scarcely able to walk, let alone walk straight.

Miz Tucker, although near her time, had nevertheless managed to bury Hiram.

'Ain't got no choice,' she'd declared when the sheriff and bank officials had arrived to evict her. 'Ain't got no money to waste on an undertaker.' She'd then terrified the bunch of them by going into labour.

Thomas soaped himself vigorously. No one had thought to dig up Hiram.

No one had questioned how he had drowned in his bath. Thomas conceded that maybe he had drowned himself, but maybe he had been assisted. Ivy had been at her wits' end having had five young ones already, and Hiram drunk and spending the money needed for feeding and bills on rot-gut whiskey.

Thomas had arrived to take Ivy away from Tucker and had been prepared to deal with Hiram should he prove difficult, but Thomas had arrived after his death.

Ivy now owned a house on the outskirts of town and made a living helping out Doc and the undertaker. Thomas saw as little of his rumbustious nieces as possible. His time was spent at his jail. He even slept in a cell, preferring to keep well away from the fractious girls.

Cavendish frowned. Irwin Kaye threatened to disrupt his peaceful existence. The new man in town would cause him problems. And Cavendish would cause problems for the Kayes simply because he was not the man they thought him to be. Cavendish had two good eyes and he used them. He could not pretend not to see wrongdoing. He would not countenance needless killing in his town.

There was a complication. Soon his contract with Salt Creek would expire. From what Bart had said it sounded as if Kaye had gained influence. He could put a spoke in the wheel and see the contract was not renewed. Cavendish was not ready to leave. He had his sister to consider. For Ivy's sake, he knew he might have to eat humble pie until that new contract was cut and dried.

★ ★ ★

Irwin Kaye had hired a new ramrod. His previous man had grown old and slow. The new man's name was Moss. Leaning back in his chair, Kaye waited for Moss, a tall, thin man of sallow complexion, to make his report. Kaye's highly polished boots rested casually on his equally highly polished mahogany desk. Kaye pushed a box of cigars towards the ramrod.

'Thanks, boss.' Moss took a cigar.

'Well!' Kaye demanded without preamble.

'Folks weren't joshing,' Moss stated. He grinned. 'It's as you've been told, Tom Cavendish is a two-bit little runt. I'd bet my boots he won't cause you any aggravation. His sister, now, she's a different matter. Miz Tucker is a formidable woman.' He guffawed, 'It's lucky for you, boss, she ain't the one wearing a star.'

'I'm not paying you to act court jester,' Kaye responded coldly. His eyes were a cold, hard blue. He was a humourless man and Moss's ramblings did not amuse him. 'Anything else I ought to know?' he snapped.

'There ain't much to tell about either of them. Cavendish applied for the job a few years back. He's a taciturn *hombre*, keeps himself to himself. When he ain't snoozing in his jail he likes to go fishing. Miz Tucker has got a sharp tongue and — '

'Damn it, Moss, I ain't interested in the man's sister!' Kaye exclaimed angrily.

'She's got six young ones. All girls, which explains why Cavendish is seldom at home,' Moss continued doggedly. 'He takes the easy way and stays out of the house. Bluntly speaking, he's a hen-pecked little runt who'll jump through hoops if you snap your fingers.'

And Patrick Kaye can rest easy, Moss thought. Sure as hell Cavendish won't be calling him to account. Cavendish would come to the boss, hat, not gun, in hand.

Kaye must have thought so also. 'Tell Cavendish I want to see him. I'll offer the runt a small retainer by way of appreciation. He'll grab it considering what he gets paid. I don't want him running too scared and quitting on us. There ain't no knowing who might fill his boots. I'll recommend the town renew his contract. From what you've said, I know he's the man to be sheriff of Salt Creek.'

Moss grinned. 'Yes, sir.' His thoughts lingered on Miz Tucker. Such were his thoughts, his ears turned red!

★   ★   ★

Ivy Tucker placed the cold meat and potato pie down on Thomas's desk. Cavendish regarded the pie gloomily.

'Humble pie, that's what I'll be eating for the next few weeks,' he observed.

'If he offers you money take it,' his sister advised. 'Never look a gift horse in the mouth as Pa would say. Just make it clear you can't be bought. Of course, he won't believe you. Not till he's looking down the barrel of your .45.'

'Hell, I hope it don't come to that,' Cavendish rejoined, starting on his pie.

'Well, that's up to Kaye. You can't sit back whilst Patrick Kaye kills folk just on account he don't like the look of them, or he's feeling mean. He's fast, so I've heard. Damn it, Thomas, there's not one man in this town who would side with you against the Kayes. I'll stand with you myself if — '

'Only that would make me a laughing stock,' Thomas interrupted, stifling a grin. 'You leave the Kayes be. We don't want to see the girls packed off to an orphanage, do we? One of us has got to stay alive.' He chewed vigorously. 'I reckon I can manage the Kayes.'

'I reckon you can,' Ivy agreed. 'And you might have to. Irwin Kaye will not respect you, nor will he fear you, until it is too late.'

Cavendish nodded. 'Maybe it won't end in a shoot out. Word will reach Salt Creek about the gun play in Garland. When he learns of my part in it that might be enough to make the Kayes toe the line and keep the law.'

'The preacher was looking for you,' Ivy informed him. 'I told him you were helping a friend in need.'

'And?' Thomas essayed.

'Said he didn't know you had any friends. I told him you had one or two. Good friends,' she added significantly.

'What did he want?' Cavendish enquired wearily. The preacher was, in fact, one of the local ranchers so nicknamed because of his liking for the scriptures.

'Rustlers. A bunch of his critters are missing. He said he'd hunt them down himself. I told him no lynching or you'd have something to say.'

'He didn't believe you?'

'I don't know,' she replied honestly. 'But he assured me he was a law-abiding man and he would fetch any taken alive back to Salt Creek. He'd see them rope dance in town, so he said.'

Cavendish nodded. 'Preacher ain't a liar, but I doubt if we'll see any live rustlers. I guess I'd best ride out and see what he's been getting up to. It might stop me thinking about Kaye.'

His sister who had been staring out of the jailhouse window shook her head. 'You won't be riding anywhere, Thomas. Unless my eyes deceive me here comes Moss, Kaye's ramrod, and he's got Patrick Kaye with him. Now that young man is heading for a fall. He can't hide behind his pa forever.'

Significantly Moss and Kaye entered the jail without the courtesy of a knock.

'Howdy, Sheriff,' Moss began affably. 'I'm Moss, Mr Kaye's ramrod. The boss would like to meet you, if it's no trouble,' he added. 'This is Patrick, Mr Kaye's son.'

Patrick smiled. He was tall, blond and good-looking. He also wore two pearl-handled guns tied low at the hip. Cavendish owned two such guns also. He kept them packed away, being reluctant to buckle on Clem's legacy believing that conspicuous weapons invited trouble.

'You must be Shorty.' Patrick continued to grin as he held out his hand. 'That's what your friends call you, unless I'm mistaken.'

'He prefers to be called Sheriff

Cavendish,' Ivy replied angrily.

'Yes, ma'am,' Moss replied hurriedly, thinking she looked about ready to throttle young Patrick Kaye. 'No offence intended, ma'am.'

There was a long silence.

'You go along, Ivy. The girls . . . ' His sister looked ready to wade in with fist and boots. He suddenly remembered Jack McGinley, a gunfighter of renown who had, many years ago, run away crying because of Ivy Cavendish as she was then.

'My pa wants to see you.' Patrick Kaye paused significantly. 'Now.'

'He'll be along when he's finished his food. You two wait outside.' Her large hand brushed against the empty jug which stood on Thomas's desk.

'We'll do that, ma'am.' Moss took Patrick's arm. She was getting ready to use the jug. Unless his eyes and instinct were deceiving him she was getting ready to wallop Patrick Kaye across the head with it.

Angrily Patrick shook off Moss's

arm, but allowed himself to be shepherded outside.

'Don't touch me again, Moss,' he
snarled.

They stood outside the office. It was
a fine day with a faint breeze. And the
breeze was needed, for tempers were
rising. Moss had an uneasy feeling that
the large woman could have wiped
Main Street with Patrick Kaye.

'No need to belittle the runt,' Moss
advised gravely. 'Your pa wants him
with us. If Cavendish bolts there'll be a
new man warming his butt on the
sheriff's chair.'

'Cavendish ain't a man. I insulted
him before his sister. He did nothing.'

'Which proves he's the man your pa
wants,' Moss argued. Just for a moment
there he'd thought Cavendish was
about to reach for his Peacemaker. Well,
he guessed, he'd have ended shooting
Cavendish.

For a moment Moss considered the
fact that no one here in Salt Creek had
actually seen the sheriff use his weapon.

Folk just assumed that Cavendish would fall short. Moss found himself wishing that Cavendish had been seen to haul iron because then Moss would know for certain just what kind of man he was dealing with. He, like the rest of them, had merely assumed and maybe they were all wrong.

Wrong assumptions led to death.

Cavendish. The name was familiar. Suddenly Moss remembered. He'd been a boy. And there'd been a killer in town: one Clem Cavendish. When Clem Cavendish had ridden out he had left two dead behind him.

Cavendish had been a big man. No way the sheriff could be related to Clem Cavendish, so Moss reasoned, thinking that if Clem Cavendish had been the sheriff of Salt Creek, Patrick Kaye would be dead. And maybe even Moss himself.

Thomas Cavendish stepped out of his office.

'Something troubling you, Moss?' he enquired mildly.

'You ain't related to Clem Cavendish by any chance?' Moss enquired.

'He was my pa,' the sheriff rejoined.

'You damn liar!' Patrick Kaye exclaimed, unable to hold back his angry, contemptuous words.

2

Irwin Kaye cordially shook Sheriff Cavendish's hand.

'I knew you were a man I could do business with,' he exclaimed with a smile.

Cavendish nodded. 'Far be it from me to stop you showing your appreciation, Mr Kaye,' he replied, aware that to argue would have cost his job.

Moss could scarcely hide his contempt. There'd been a moment outside the office when he had thought he had misjudged Sheriff Thomas Cavendish. Something dangerous had flared in Cavendish's eyes before he had shrugged and responded laconically, 'You're right, Patrick I was joshing. Let's not keep Mr Kaye waiting. I'd hazard he's not the most patient of men.'

Cavendish was right, Moss had

nodded. 'Let's ride,' he had ordered curtly. As the three had ridden out of town, Patrick Kaye had sniggered openly.

Irwin Kaye laughed easily. 'Appreciation! I like that, Cavendish. Appreciation eh!'

'You understand, of course,' Cavendish observed impassively, 'that as an elected lawman I'm duty bound to uphold the law without fear or favour.'

A choking sound escaped Moss. Conscious of his boss's eye upon him he smothered his laughter.

'You're not saying you don't want my money, are you, Cavendish?' Kaye pretended to be aggrieved.

'Not at all, Mr Kaye. It's much appreciated.'

Moss turned away sickened at the sight of the grovelling little runt.

Not so Irwin Kaye. 'Good man!' he exclaimed, patting the sheriff soundly on the back. 'Good man. I knew I could count on you. I knew we would see eye to eye on a good many matters.'

'There's the matter of my contract,

Mr Kaye,' Cavendish reminded. 'There's been talk in town about it not being renewed. So my sister tells me.'

'Leave the matter in my hands, Sheriff Cavendish,' Kaye replied pompously. 'I'll sort matters out. Your new contract will be ready and waiting in a day or so. You just drop in on Jake McNaught. I can vouch that you won't be disappointed.'

'Thank you, sir,' Cavendish rejoined. His eyes were lowered. 'I appreciate your interest.'

Kaye nodded. As far as he was concerned the business with the sheriff was concluded. 'I'm sure you have matters in town needing your attention, Sheriff. When I need you I'll let you know.'

'I'm sure you will, Mr Kaye,' Cavendish answered drily. Moss was already opening the door. 'I'll see myself out.'

Kaye turned to his son. 'Well, I guess we won't be hearing a word about the drifter you blasted. But a man has to have a reason to kill. You can't pick a fight because you don't like a man's looks. Now say, for example, that drifter had been as fast as Jack McGinley you'd be a dead man.'

'Jack McGinley!' Moss exclaimed. 'He ain't in these parts is he, boss?'

'Not so I've heard,' Irwin Kaye answered, thinking that Moss could be slow-witted at times. 'I'm using McGinley as an example. What I'm trying to say, Son, is that you should know your man before you pick a fight. You've a way to go before you're McGinley's equal.'

'I ain't scared of McGinley,' Patrick Kaye rejoined. 'I believe I can beat him.'

His father's clenched fist struck the desk. 'Get the hell out of here, you young fool. You haven't listened to a word I've been saying. And leave Shorty be. I'm the one jerking Cavendish's leash. Don't forget it. Last thing I need is a dead lawman.'

Patrick Kaye smirked. 'Yes, Pa,' he agreed, as he ambled out, unmoved by his pa's fury.

'You keep an eye on my boy whilst he's in town,' Kaye ordered his ramrod.

Moss rubbed his chin thoughtfully. Patrick Kaye was a mean-hearted little varmint. 'Hell, boss, I ain't a match for Jack McGinley. You'd need a top gun to best McGinley.'

Kaye cussed. 'Forget about McGinley.' He was sorry he had mentioned the hired gun's name.

★　★　★

Thomas Cavendish rode away from the meeting knowing he had belittled himself. He was ready to explode. 'Yes, sir no sir,' he muttered. 'Hell, that contract better be ready soon.' He had a hunch that he and Irwin Kaye were on a collision course. Just as Duffy and Colonel Parker had been on a collision course. The arrogant and over-confident Colonel Parker hadn't been able to see it. Irwin Kaye, Cavendish had soon recognized was just such a man as Colonel Parker.

Cavendish sighed. If only he did not need this job he would have left Irwin Kaye in no doubt as to how matters stood. Ivy's girls were a trial, but as their uncle he had a responsibility to see them grown.

Ivy was talking about sending the eldest one East to boarding-school. She had some crazy idea of tapping McGinley for a loan. True, the two had shared a desk in school, but Ivy had often walloped young Jack McGinley. Surely Jack McGinley would split his sides laughing if he heard from Ivy Cavendish as she had been.

Thomas himself had never liked Jack McGinley. But McGinley was preferable to the Kayes. Especially Patrick Kaye. McGinley killed for money. He would never pick a fight because he did not like the look of an *hombre*. Patrick Kaye was heading for a fall and the big ramrod wouldn't be able to save young Patrick when that day came.

★　★　★

'I see the town has raised your salary,' Lawyer Jake McNaught observed with a disapproving snort. 'You can thank Irwin Kaye. You get on out there and lick those polished boots and — '

'And would you stand beside me if I had to shoot it out with Irwin?' Cavendish enquired. McNaught's expression was the answer he needed. McNaught fell silent.

Just then yells and hoots broke out on Main Street putting paid to further discussion. Cavendish thinned his lips. He had a pretty good idea of what the cause of the disturbance might be.

'What in tarnation!' McNaught heaved his bulk up from his chair and waddled towards the window, his huge belly threatening to burst out of his pants. 'Goddamnit,' he exclaimed, 'it's the preacher and he's taken a prisoner. A female to boot! Dressed like a man. What do you say about that, Sheriff?'

Cavendish ignored the damn fool question. He signed the contracts. Two. One copy for himself; one for the town.

It was done: his job was safe. They could not terminate his employment no matter what Irwin Kaye might wish. His monthly stipend was secured. Now he could rest easy.

He wasn't worried. He knew his own worth. He was as fast as McGinley. Indeed McGinley had once suggested that Thomas hire out his gun. Cavendish grinned. His sister had thrown a full coffee pot at McGinley's head. Fortunately McGinley had ducked.

At present she was worrying that he might hesitate at a crucial moment. Cavendish had reassured her a hundred times he would not hesitate when it came to pulling the trigger. He'd also reminded her that Duffy had no cause for complaint. But he might have known he could not get the better of Ivy Tucker.

'And how do you feel about Garland?' she'd asked.

He had fallen into the trap. 'Damnation, Ivy, I feel as though I've seen enough killing to last me a lifetime!' he'd exclaimed.

'Precisely,' she'd exclaimed triumphantly. 'You felt sorry for the men you killed.'

'Well, I can't help that,' he'd replied. 'I feel there was no purpose to their dying.'

'You're wasting your goddamn time, Thomas,' she had exclaimed. 'Feeling sorry for men planted six feet under won't help them none, and it won't help you. Fact is, I'd say it was dangerous . . .'

'No one will gun me down if I can prevent it,' he had reassured her. 'I'll pull the trigger pretty damn fast if need arises.'

'Ain't you interested?' McNaught enquired irritably, interrupting Cavendish's thoughts. 'You have a prisoner, man. A widelooper. And a handsome female from what I can see. At least she would be if she was cleaned up and rigged out decent. Lord, Cavendish,' the garrulous lawyer continued without a pause, 'I declare, upon occasion you look like you've lost your wits.'

Cavendish ignored the insult. He wasn't happy about having a female in his jail.

'Show some enthusiasm, man!' McNaught urged.

'Why should I?' Cavendish asked.

'Hell, if you don't know that, Sheriff . . . ' McNaught guffawed. 'If she was riding with a bunch of wideloopers, well, it figures she's . . . '

To his annoyance, Cavendish, evidently uninterested in the lawyer's opinion, was heading for the door.

Cavendish stepped out on to Main Street leaving McNaught to follow on behind him.

'The whore of Babylon can rot in your jail until the circuit judge arrives!' Preacher exclaimed. He licked his lips. 'Her end is a foregone conclusion. We'll hang her.'

'Maybe,' Cavendish shrugged. 'You sure you ain't been out in the sun too long, Preacher?'

'No. Why?'

'You go to hell, you . . . ' the woman

cried, a stream of profanities issuing from her mouth.

Cavendish stepped up to the wagon where she lay. He saw she had a black eye and bruised cheek. She was bound hand and foot. She spat at him. And swore again.

Cavendish stepped back.

'Tough measures are called for, wouldn't you say, Sheriff?' Adam Eden a prosperous rancher jeered.

Cavendish, spotting one of his nieces lurking on the edge of the crowd, beckoned. He whispered something to Lottie and she sped away.

Hell, Cavendish thought, the men gathered around the wagon reminded him of a pack of jackals. A good many had a peculiar glint in their eye which he did not care for.

'Haul her inside, boys,' Preacher ordered.

'Don't none of you touch my prisoner,' Cavendish warned.

'So you want to haul her in yourself, do you?' a waddy jeered. 'Well, I reckon you can manage that.'

'Well, you reckon wrong,' Cavendish rejoined. With relief he saw his sister approaching.

'While I'm in charge of a female prisoner,' he declared loudly, 'Miz Tucker can serve as my deputy. Paid for by the town. As set out in my new contract.' Few noticed he emphasized the word *new*. Lawyer McNaught noticed, however. He looked at Cavendish speculatively thinking that really Salt Creek knew very little about Thomas Cavendish. He had a sudden hunch they were about to find out.

'You can't hire a woman,' Adam Eden blustered.

'I can hire who I damn well want if I deem it necessary,' Cavendish stated calmly. 'You check with Mr Kaye,' he couldn't resist adding.

Irwin Kaye had explained the situation. His men would double as deputies as and when he Irwin Kaye deemed it necessary. Needless to say, Cavendish had no intention of deputizing Kaye's gun-happy crew.

'You're making a fool of yourself, man,' Adam Eden bellowed, his irritation evident. 'You go on home, woman. I'll have one of my men haul that Jezebel inside if you're — '

'No!' Cavendish squared up to Eden. 'I'm the Sheriff of Salt Creek. What I say goes. You might not like it, but there it is. Now I'd like you folk to disperse. The show's over. Ivy, you get the prisoner inside and settled in.'

'You jumped up, little . . . ' Eden's angry words died away as he stared into the muzzle of Cavendish's gun. He hadn't even realized Cavendish had intended to haul iron, nor how fast the sheriff was.

'Next time you insult me you'd better be prepared to step out on to Main Street and back your words with action. It's my policy to shoot to kill. So anyone who muffs it first time round doesn't get a second chance to plug me. Best way, I find: it keeps life simple. Now, I ain't a man to harbour a grudge and if you folk will disperse I'll overlook the fact that there are some amongst you who are intent upon hampering me carrying out my duty.'

Eden blanched. 'You're crazy, Cavendish. But as you say you are the law,' he added in an attempt to save face. 'I respect the law.' He turned on his heels and strode away.

'Salt Creek has always been a law-abiding town. That's a mighty fast draw, Cavendish. I'd say you are almost as fast as McGinley. I saw that devil's spawn kill a man once! That's right, ma'am, you get that she-devil inside. I never thought it fitting that you be in charge of a female prisoner, Cavendish. I was for hanging her there and then . . . '

'And a good job you didn't Preacher,' Cavendish interrupted, wondering what had got into this normally taciturn man. 'I cannot countenance lynching. If you had done, I would have been duty bound to arrest and charge you. I am sure you understand about duty!'

37

Preacher laughed, but the laugh was forced.

Cavendish watched the crowd disperse. He kept his gun drawn. Not that he anticipated trouble. His ability had impressed them. None of them were eager to challenge him now. He could handle Salt Creek. He sure as hell hoped that when Kaye heard that Salt Creek's lawman didn't wear a .45 for decoration Kaye would tread carefully.

Having no desire to face his prisoner, Cavendish headed for the livery barn. Old Bart Parker kept a stone jug and Cavendish was mindful to share the contents of that jug. The truth was that he didn't care for the idea of seeing a female dangle from the gallows. She was young and pretty. He might be a lawman but ... Hell, his natural inclination was to allow an escape. After all, losing a female prisoner didn't count for much; it was not like losing a real desperado. Trouble was if he let her out now, Preacher would raise a hue and cry. Preacher might be a religious man, but he sure as hell wasn't a merciful one.

Cavendish sighed. The nearer he got to the livery barn the more appealing Bart Parker's jug became.

★ ★ ★

'So how come you left Colonel Parker?' Moss's eyes narrowed. 'I heard tell the colonel pays real well. What happened? Sacked were you?'

'No, sir,' the waddy replied. He shrugged. 'You're way behind times, Ramrod. The colonel is dead. And his boys. Dead and planted.'

'What's that you're saying!' The man had Moss's full attention.

'All done legally,' the cowhand explained. 'The colonel broke the law. Ain't no one could say he didn't. Duffy was slow to act, but when he finally got his butt out of his office all hell broke loose. Hell, Cavendish is a cold-hearted little runt, ain't he?'

'Cavendish? What the hell has he got

to do with it?' Moss demanded somewhat perplexed.

'Well, he was there in Garland. Standing alongside Duffy. Fact is, it was Cavendish who took off the colonel's head. Cooked himself a meal, so I heard tell, in the colonel's kitchen once the shooting was over. Eggs, steak and bacon so Lopez the cook said.'

'You come with me. The boss has got to hear about this,' Moss grated. Gut instinct was telling him Irwin Kaye had made one hell of a mistake, and he, Moss, had been instrumental in helping Irwin make that mistake. Thomas Cavendish was not what the town thought him to be. Moss recalled Kaye's last order, 'Get that goddamn lawyer to draw up Shorty's new contract.' Kaye had guffawed. 'We don't want to lose the man now, do we?' he had jested.

Moss had a hunch that once Kaye heard what had happened in Garland he would not be laughing.

'What the hell do you want?' Kaye

did not trouble to hide his irritation. He sat behind his big desk, paperwork spread out in front of him, a cigar clamped between his teeth and a glass of whiskey at his right hand. 'Can't you see I'm busy, man?

'This can't wait,' Moss rejoined. 'There's something you ought to know. It concerns Cavendish. Seems he might not be the little coward you think him. He could be one dangerous *hombre*!'

'What the hell are you talking about?' Kaye stubbed out his cigar.

Succinctly the waddy related the events which had occurred.

'The hell you say!' Kaye roared. The whiskey glass shattered in his hand.

'Guess I'll wait outside,' the waddy muttered and beat a hasty retreat.

'Seems Cavendish has a talent for killing,' Moss observed unhappily, aware that his job was on the line.

'Patrick has gone into town,' Kaye stated and there was an odd note in his voice which Moss had never heard before.

'And knowing Patrick he ain't going to walk on egg shells around Cavendish,' Moss voiced his boss's thought. 'Could be lethal if Patrick met the real Thomas Cavendish.' He paused. 'Why has Patrick gone into town?' Moss had no business asking, but the boss seemed unduly troubled.

'Foolishness. The boys have been talking about the woman Cavendish has shut up in the jail and — '

'Patrick had a mind to pay her a visit,' Moss concluded. There had been talk in the bunk-house about how a farm girl had hanged herself on account of Patrick Kaye, Irwin having brought some of his old crew with him. 'Well, I'd best get into town. We don't know for sure whether Cavendish will challenge Patrick.'

Irwin Kaye rose to his feet. 'I'll ride with you!'

Moss shook his head. 'Folk joke about Patrick hiding behind your coat tails,' he advised. 'Let me handle this. Patrick won't thank you if you charge in like a bull in a china shop.'

Irwin, Moss reflected, could make things a damn sight worse than they need be. Privately, Moss was of the opinion that if Cavendish was capable of taking off the colonel's head he would not baulk at dealing with young Patrick Kaye. Prudently, Moss kept that thought to himself.

If there was trouble with Cavendish the Kayes had only themselves to blame. Patrick Kaye was out of his head and so was Irwin. This wasn't the way to test Cavendish's loyalty.

*   *   *

From the way his prisoner cussed him, any one hearing her would assume that he was the one who had hunted her down and brought her in to face justice. Wearily, Cavendish closed his ears. Irma her name was, so Ivy had said.

When Irma finally ran out of steam he raised his voice. 'You yell all you want Miss Irma. Noise don't bother me none. But I don't advise you to let Miz Tucker hear you. She's liable to make you eat soap.'

Cavendish was at his desk. The adjoining door between the office and cell block was open, but he would not be going anywhere near his prisoner. All conversation was being conducted through the open door.

'What's so funny?' she hollered.

'Just remembering the time Miz Tucker made Jack McGinley eat soap.'

'McGinley? You know McGinley?' She was impressed. 'I don't believe you.'

'I ain't a liar ma'am. Fact is, they were at school at the time.'

'You were his friend?'

'Nope. We never got on. Last thing I want to see is McGinley in my town.'

'But why would he come here?'

'Fact is, Ivy's written to him. Behind my back. I ain't well pleased and . . . '

The door of his office was thrust open putting an end to their conversation. Patrick Kaye swaggered into the office. Two waddies followed at his heels.

'Good day, Shorty,' Kaye jeered.

Cavendish smelt the whiskey fumes.

'Good day, Patrick.' He sensed trouble coming his way.

'Only my friends call me Patrick. You ain't my friend, Shorty.'

'That's right. I am not your friend.' Cavendish's voice was expressionless, 'And now we've established I ain't your friend would you care to tell me what this is about? How can I help you?'

'You take a stroll round town, Cavendish.' Reaching in his pocket Patrick Kaye pulled out a coin. He placed the coin on the desk. 'Buy yourself a beer or two. Don't hurry back.'

'Why not?' Thomas enquired mildly. He guessed he knew why. Patrick Kaye's words confirmed his hunch.

'Why, I aim to get acquainted with your prisoner, Shorty. You ain't having all the fun. I want that woman.'

'I ain't had no fun. And you ain't

getting your fun in my jail house. I draw the line at hanky-panky, Kaye. And if you persist I guess I'll have to remind you that I'm the Sheriff of Salt Creek. I can thank your pa for that. But I ain't going to thank him by obliging you. No way. Now get out.'

3

'You don't know my pa,' Patrick warned. 'You cross me, you cross my pa. No one crosses Irwin Kaye and gets away with it. I want that woman and I mean to have her. Me, and the boys.'

'I don't give a damn what you want.' Rising to his feet Cavendish placed his hands on the desk. This foolishness had to be ended pretty damn quick or he would be forced to shoot all three of them. 'Head on over to the Golden Garter,' he advised. 'You'll find plenty of women willing to oblige. I'll forget about this conversation.'

'The hell you will!' Patrick Kaye shouted angrily. 'Goddamn it, Cavendish, are you stupid? I want the woman you've got locked away.'

'Well, you can't have her. I'm a lawman and from where I'm standing you aim to break the law.'

'Damn it, you took my pa's money,' Patrick accused. 'You know what he said.' Patrick Kaye thrust his face forward.

Cavendish noted the face was turning red with rage. He fixed his eyes on Kaye's aristocratic nose. Cavendish had once seen a painting of two French aristocrats so he recognized an aristocratic nose when he saw one.

' 'You go ahead and enjoy yourself, son'. That's what my pa said. And by God I aim to do just that!'

Cavendish had never figured Irwin Kaye for a fool but maybe he was wrong. 'Well, I guess I ain't got a choice.'

Patrick Kaye gave a triumphant grin. 'I knew you'd see sense, Shorty,' he replied insultingly.

'You stink, Cavendish. You yellow-bellied, no-account bastard!' Irma hollered, but Cavendish recognized the fear in her defiant words.

He smiled pleasantly. 'You're a hot-head boy. Me I've always been told — ' the sentence broke off abruptly as Cavendish, acting before Kaye realized his intention, grabbed Kaye's ears. As Patrick Kaye was hauled over the desk towards the sheriff, Cavendish's head shot forward and, with a sickening thud, the two foreheads collided.

Immediately, Cavendish released the boy. He himself felt none the worse for the encounter, but Patrick Kaye fell backwards, groaning. With a thump he landed on the floor and there he stayed, eyes glazed and vacant.

A .45 appeared in Cavendish's hand as the two waddies gawked opened-mouthed, stunned by this unexpected turn of events. Their expressions made it abundantly clear that they had not expected this to happen.

'I've a hard head,' Cavendish concluded, with a wolfish smile. 'And if you two boys want to keep on breathing you won't cause me trouble. Now tote that garbage out of here before I dispose of him permanently.'

'Yes, sir,' the older of the two

nodded. There was respect in his eyes. 'Irwin Kaye ain't going to care for this,' he observed quite unnecessarily.

Cavendish nodded. 'I know that. Now haul that piece of offal out of my office before I decide to send him home to his pa in a box.' The play-acting was over. Cavendish was through acting the part of an affable clown.

He was fully aware that Irwin Kaye would not forgive him for the way in which Patrick had been humiliated. But the young fool had only himself to blame. Nor could Cavendish forget how Patrick had taken such pleasure in killing the luckless drifter.

Cavendish sat at his desk. He reached for his pen figuring it was time to set down what had occurred. Since becoming Salt Creek's lawman he had been penning his memoirs, *Memories of a Frontier Sheriff*. Trouble was, not much had happened during his time in Salt Creek, Cavendish therefore had been forced to resort to his imagination.

'You've got to let me out of here,

Cavendish,' his prisoner hollered. 'I'll make it worth your while. Damn it, Cavendish, I don't want to hang. I'll do anything to escape that neck-tie party. Anything! Do you hear me, Tom Cavendish!'

'I hear you, Miss Irma,' Cavendish replied. There was a sour taste in his mouth. He imagined her dancing at the end of a rope. 'I don't want to see you hang, Miss Irma.' To hell with his oath and to hell with upholding the law without fear or favour.

'If you could see your way to letting me go I'd be real grateful, Tom, real grateful,' she cried, trying to control her terror.

'I'm a lawman, Irma. I can't be bribed,' Cavendish began, meaning to explain he would see she did not hang without taking up her offer.

'You don't sound too sure, Tom. Come on in here and we can discuss the matter.'

Cavendish locked the jailhouse door. Whether Miss Irma was grateful made no difference. He would see her safe in any event.

'Real grateful!' she yelled again.

'I reckon I have to decline,' Cavendish replied regretfully, thinking that she was a fine-looking woman who sorely tempted him, but only a low-down polecat would take advantage of her dire situation. He had his self-respect; he had his principles. And he aimed to keep his self-respect and principles.

'Why you sanctimonious little runt! You'd be the last man I'd want. I wouldn't spit on you if you was on fire,' she screeched.

Cavendish wasn't about to let her get away with insulting him. To hell with his principles.

He moved towards the door which separated the cells from his office.

'I've changed my mind, Irma. You can show your gratitude if you've a mind to.'

'You go to hell, Cavendish. I don't trust you. You'd let me swing in any event.'

'That ain't so, Miss Irma. And I've just saved you from . . . '

'If you're expecting thanks you ain't going to get it.'

Cavendish retreated knowing that there was no reasoning with her. He was determined on the last word. 'You'll come round, Miss Irma. I know you will.'

'Has it occurred to you, Thomas Cavendish, that you may not be around very much longer? You called that varmint offal . . . '

'Well, so he is.'

'And pretty soon the whole town will know it. The only way Kaye can save face is to get rid of you one way or another.'

'You let me worry about that, Miss Irma.'

'There's one thing I can't abide, Cavendish.'

'What might that be, Miss Irma?'

'A man who worries.'

Cavendish slammed the door separating the cells from his office. He retreated to his desk. Miss Irma was damn right about one thing: Irwin Kaye would be out to get him and that was for sure.

★ ★ ★

'You're fired. I put store in your word, Moss. I trusted your judgement. You let me down. I need a ramrod with savvy and you ain't got any. Get your gear and get off my ranch.'

Moss clutched his hat.

'You're stupid, Moss. Plain stupid. You know that?' Irwin ranted.

'Not so stupid I'd look for a woman in a jail cell,' Moss replied. 'And not so stupid that I don't know if you cross horns with Sheriff Cavendish you'll lose Mr Kaye. I guess you're doing me a favour.'

'Get out of my sight. You make me sick,' Irwin snarled.

Moss headed for the bunkhouse. He'd met the hands bringing Patrick Kaye home and had returned with them. That Patrick wasn't dead said much for Cavendish's restraint.

Irwin had not shown restraint and rather than admit that he was to blame for Patrick's damaged head, Irwin was piling the blame on Moss.

But it wasn't all bad, Moss reflected. Fired by Irwin he was now free to pay court to Ivy Tucker. There was just something about that woman that attracted him and . . .

And Moss thinking of Ivy Tucker was taken by surprise when three of the men jumped him and proceeded to lay into him with boots and fists.

'This is for Patrick,' one of them yelled, when the beating was concluded. The speaker was Eastman, one of the men brought to Salt Creek by the Kayes. 'And you can give Cavendish a message from Mr Kaye: tell him to get the hell out of Salt Creek or he's a dead man.'

★ ★ ★

Hammering at the jailhouse door disturbed Cavendish's reflections. Miss

Irma still had not come round. Cavendish's hand dropped automatically to the butt of his .45.

'State your business,' he hollered, ready for trouble and half expecting to find Irwin Kaye at the jailhouse door.

'It's me, Bart Parker!' a voice responded.

'Are you alone?'

'Irwin and the crew aren't here with me if that's what you're asking,' Bart responded. 'But I've got Moss with me.'

Cavendish drew his .45. The door opened abruptly and Bart found himself staring into the mouth of the .45.

'I ain't here to make trouble,' Moss croaked through swollen lips.

'Says he got run over by a train,' Bart jested, as Cavendish stepped back allowing them both access.

'Your days in Salt Creek are numbered, Sheriff!' Moss mumbled. 'Irwin Kaye says to get out of town.' Moss groaned.

Cavendish shrugged. 'Your fool of a

boss ought to be down on his knees thanking me for not blasting his damn fool son.'

'Irwin don't see it that way. And I've been fired,' Moss informed him with a grimace.

Cavendish grinned. 'That figures. You recommended me to Irwin!'

'I made a mistake.' Moss groaned again.

'So, has Preacher posted lookouts on the trails out of town?' Cavendish asked, his thoughts returning to Irma.

Moss nodded. 'He's got the town surrounded.'

'So why are you here?' Cavendish enquired, not liking what he'd heard. 'Not to tell me you've been fired and not to tell me you'll stand with me against the Kayes.'

'I aim to stay alive!' Moss declared. 'This ain't my fight!'

'And?'

'And I'm telling you plainly I intend to call upon Miz Tucker.'

Cavendish almost choked on his

mouthful of coffee.

'So what do you say?' Moss sounded as though he expected trouble.

Cavendish thought of Hiram Tucker and his untimely demise. He nodded. 'You go ahead, Moss. My sister is a strong-minded woman. She'll do what she wants in any event.'

'McGinley's coming to town!' Bart broke in. 'He's looking for you.'

'I doubt it,' Cavendish rejoined.

'Damn it, Cavendish!' Bart yelled. 'Don't be a fool. McGinley has been hired to kill you.' Bart glared at Moss. 'Has Irwin hired McGinley?' he demanded.

Moss shook his head. 'Not to my knowledge. What are you aiming to do, Sheriff?'

'I aim to finish my coffee, if you two varmints could get out of my office,' Cavendish replied, thinking that soon all of Salt Creek would believe McGinley was after his hide. 'And tell that damn telegraph clerk, Pole, to keep his mouth shut. He ain't supposed to broadcast telegram contents. I ain't never cared for that man!'

'Watch your back, Cavendish, or you may not be around when McGinley hits Salt Creek,' Bart advised. He eyed Cavendish, knowing how Cavendish felt about having a female hanged in Salt Creek.

'Judge Reginald Gough is on his way,' Bart advised. 'He'll be here real soon. I reckon that's why Preacher has got his men around the town. He was the first to know. Had some kind of arrangement with Pole, I guess. If you're thinking of sneaking her out of town best forget it.'

Moss nodded his agreement. 'It can't be done.'

'Hell!' Cavendish exclaimed savagely. Preacher had forestalled him. Damn them both, Preacher *and* Pole. He took a deep breath and forced himself to calm knowing that rage was fatal. Rage got a man killed.

This two-bit town was not going to hang Miss Irma. It was up to him to save her and he aimed to do it.

Cavendish recognized that he was not the lawman he had thought himself to be. Things had changed. It was no longer his intention to uphold the law without fear or favour. When it came to choosing between Miss Irma and the law, Miss Irma won hands down. Not that he expected any gratitude from her. A cussing is what he would get for she'd say he ought to have got her out of town sooner. And he would have if he had not believed Preacher would start a hue and cry.

'Go get your jug, Bart,' he advised. 'I reckon I'm in need.'

'No!' Bart was emphatic. 'You need a clear head and a fast gun hand. My stone jug can't help you. But they say the Devil looks after his own: he looked after Clem Cavendish and I guess he'll look after you.'

Thomas Cavendish was left wondering whether Bart had been joshing. With the oldster it was hard to tell.

* * *

Reginald Gough sat with his hands folded. His expression was calm. He was an impressive-looking man which was just as it should be for he was also an important man: a man with the power of life and death.

He knew his duty. The fact that he was known on the circuit as the hanging judge did not trouble him. Gough had but the one fear and that fear was that one day he might find Jack McGinley in the dock before him. Gough feared McGinley and he feared to try and rid himself of McGinley. It had been twenty years since he had seen McGinley and yet he thought of him every day. He was the one man who could prevent him from becoming Senator Gough.

And then his worst nightmare was realized: McGinley strolled into the foyer of the hotel.

Gough felt a tightening across his chest. By virtue of his profession McGinley should have been long dead. Truly the Devil looked after his own.

That McGinley had survived for so many years said much for his skill with a Colt revolver.

McGinley winked.

Twenty years ago, Gough, a rising young attorney, had hired McGinley.

Beside Judge Gough, his daughter, Joyce, simpered, believing the handsome stranger had winked at her.

'Who is that man?' the judge's wife Jane hissed.

'No one of importance,' Gough replied, wishing Hell would open and claim McGinley.

'He's coming our way.' Joyce blushed prettily.

McGinley bowed. 'Judge Gough,' he drawled, as though they were long-standing acquaintances.

'I don't know you, sir.' Gough forced the words through clenched teeth, but his hand was shaking and McGinley had seen it.

'I feel sure we've met before, Judge.' McGinley's voice was courteous. 'My name is Jack McGinley.'

'I've heard of you, McGinley,' Judge Gough snapped, 'but our paths have never crossed.'

'I'm sure it will come to me one day,' McGinley taunted. He smiled at the ladies. 'The fact is, Judge, you hanged an acquaintance of mine. *Hombre* by the name of Egan.'

'That man deserved to die,' Mrs Gough exclaimed angrily. 'He was a murderer.'

'I'm sure he did, ma'am,' McGinley agreed soothingly. 'Did you watch the hanging, ma'am?' he enquired politely.

The woman gasped with indignation.

'No offence, ma'am, but there's some that find a hanging mighty interesting. I've heard tell there's a female wide-looper in Salt Creek awaiting your attention, Judge.' McGinley paused. 'I'm headed for Salt Creek myself.' He bowed. 'Maybe I'll be riding in the very same stage as yourself, Judge, and your good ladies.'

'If you'll excuse us, McGinley, we have business to attend to.' Gough, who by now felt slightly sick, shepherded his family back upstairs.

'We'll have us the opportunity to become better acquainted,' McGinley called softly, eying the bustles on the ladies' dresses. He wondered whether it was possible to become better acquainted with Mrs and Miss Gough. It would be a challenge. And there was nothing more Jack enjoyed than a challenge.

Gough might boil but there was nothing he could do, not if he wanted that seat in Congress. McGinley kept up with the news when he could and Judge Reginald Gough had always interested him. Gough was a varmint through and through. And the fact that such a varmint as Gough now judged others Jack McGinley found highly amusing.

He had also found it amusing to hear from Ivy Tucker after all this time. He'd kept tabs on Ivy and Tom. Tom would have been a disappointment to Clem for Tom had turned lawman. Hiram's demise would have redeemed Ivy: she'd shown herself a true Cavendish.

Despite what he suspected about Hiram, Jack aimed to get better acquainted with Ivy.

He left the hotel. Salt Creek was going to prove an interesting place.

★   ★   ★

Thomas Cavendish moved his prisoner just before dawn broke. He moved her into his sister's house thinking that the Salt Creek jail was no longer safe for Irma.

Life in Salt Creek had always been uninteresting until now but things were livening up. Cavendish did not allow himself to dwell upon what might happen. All that he allowed himself to admit was that events in Salt Creek were liable to provide the town's inhabitants with a good deal of interest.

Irwin Kaye was not a patient man and he would be making his move pretty damn soon.

Throughout the day, Cavendish stayed in his office. Ivy, who came over with his meals, reported that the town reminded her of a kettle ready to whistle. Folk were just watching and waiting she said.

'And you remember,' she declared, as she stepped out the door, 'you just remember you don't have a friend in this town!'

'Well, Bart offered,' Cavendish said. 'but the old coot doesn't see too good.' He shrugged. 'If I get killed, do what you can for Irma.'

'That's defeatist talk, Thomas Cavendish. Pa would be ashamed of you.'

Cavendish shook his head. 'I'm not the man Pa was.'

'Maybe you're a better man; I guess Pa wouldn't have worried about old Bart Parker. But Pa taught you everything he knew — '

'And I ought to be able to deal with Salt Creek,' Cavendish replied, even managing a smile.

That evening when he stepped out of

his office he remembered the words spoken earlier. He found the sidewalks deserted, for night had fallen upon the town. Light spilled from Salt Creek's two saloons, pools of light in the darkness, which would draw in any new arrivals like magnets. From inside the saloons came the sounds of music and laughter.

'Hell, Sheriff, if I were you I'd be quaking in my boots and ... ' the drunk who had just emerged from the nearest saloon lurched along the sidewalk towards Cavendish who had just commenced his nightly patrol. Whiskey fumes enveloped the shambling figure of Mooney.

Cavendish shook his head knowing that pretty soon Mooney would begin to roar about green fields and soft rain the like of which were not seen in this godforsaken dustbowl.

Last time Mooney had been drunk he had shouted about little people who would be sure to make Sheriff Thomas Cavendish feel right at home.

Cavendish had ignored the drunk. He had not shut Mooney's mouth as many would have done.

Mooney reached the diminutive lawman.

'Hell, I feel . . .' With a groan Mooney spewed his victuals over Cavendish's newly polished boots. Boots polished to please Miss Irma who had remarked his boots were a disgrace.

Cavendish's restraint evaporated. He glared down upon Mooney, now down on his hands and knees and oblivious to the danger from an irate Cavendish.

★   ★   ★

Eastman and Decker had entered Salt Creek on foot having left their mounts tethered a short distance from the town's perimeter. If their horses were not at the livery barn, if needs be they could deny they were ever in town this night.

When Cavendish had begun his patrol, the two had been waiting impatiently in a stinking alleyway across the street from the jail. They'd been taking bets on whether Cavendish would have the guts to show his nose. If not they were resolved to keep trying.

The appearance of Mooney had been a distraction. Both watched with mirth as Mooney vomited his guts over Cavendish's boots. That occurrence would cheer the Kayes no end. When the men had ridden out, Irwin had been ranting that Cavendish reminded him of a cockerel on a dung heap.

'Now!' Decker hissed. He lifted his rifle, sighted on Cavendish and . . .

'You damn bum, Mooney.' Cavendish kicked Mooney soundly on the butt deriving great satisfaction as his foot thudded against flesh. 'I ought to fill you full of holes . . . '

Mooney howled.

'But I've got a better idea!'

As Cavendish dropped to his knees intent on pressing Mooney's face into a pile of horse droppings, Decker fired.

4

'Jesus save us!' Mooney cried as he struggled desperately to free himself from beneath the sheriff. Freeing himself from Cavendish's weight, Mooney, on all fours, scrabbled crab-like away.

Cavendish lay still. He played dead, hoping that whoever had fired might not realize the shot had missed.

Decker stepped from the shadow. He was pretty sure that the slug must have hit the sheriff. However, he intended to put a second slug into Cavendish for good measure.

Goddamn it, Cavendish thought, I ought to be dead. On his belly! He waited, knowing that he had but the one chance to save himself from certain death. His head moved slightly and his eyes focused upon the shadowy figure across the street.

The one became two as the man's

companion stepped out to join him.

'Get on with it,' Eastman hissed.

Cavendish's slug struck Decker squarely in the chest an instant before Decker's trigger finger was due to tighten. Decker dropped instantly, his .45 discharging harmlessly.

'What the hell!' Eastman exclaimed. Those were the last words he spoke, for Cavendish's second slug took off the top of his head. It was typical of this town, Cavendish thought, that no one had come out yet to investigate.

Mooney staggered into the Golden Garter, the saloon from which he had been ejected but a short while ago. At first no one paid heed to his gabbling but when a further two shots rang out customers moved towards the batwings, although no one was fool enough to go rushing out.

Cavendish stood up and wisely kept his .45 in his hand. His hunch had proved correct. That skunk, Irwin Kaye, had not allowed time to elapse before seeking to dispose of Salt

Creek's lawman.

Men were beginning to emerge from the saloons now, many of them drunk.

'What the hell!' a voice yelled.

'Hell,' a voice exclaimed excitedly, 'the sheriff has blasted two of Irwin Kaye's men!'

The speaker had not even looked to confirm the two dead men were Irwin's employees. Cavendish hadn't been the only one expecting Kaye to launch a murder attempt. No one troubled to enquire about his well-being. He could be bleeding to death for all any of these bums cared.

'Irwin Kaye sure as hell ain't going to be pleased,' a third voice commented inanely.

Cavendish had had enough. So much for the citizens of Salt Creek, he thought. He headed back towards his office shutting his ears to the excited gabbling behind him. He slammed the door and locked it and ignored the knocks which came later.

'Hell! What happened?' Bart Parker

hammered on the door.

'Get lost, Bart,' Cavendish yelled.

'Are you going after Irwin Kaye?' Bart hollered.

Cavendish did not trouble to reply. Silence ensued and then Bart was gone. Cavendish sat in the darkness thinking that tonight's failure would not deter a man such as Irwin Kaye. He did not need to go after Irwin. Cavendish had a hunch that events would spiral and pretty soon get out of hand. He'd let Irwin make the next move. Whatever Irwin threw at him he could handle.

Cavendish found satisfaction in envisaging Irwin's reaction tomorrow when the two dead men were toted home. Maybe Irwin would even sweat awhile wondering whether the law, in the shape of Cavendish, would appear to ask him to account for his men, or maybe not.

Cavendish found he really didn't give a damn about Irwin Kaye, or Salt Creek. No fool, Cavendish realized that if he sought to raise a posse with which to confront Irwin he would be unlikely to find one man willing to ride alongside him. It was a sobering thought.

*   *   *

Ivy Tucker left the jailhouse. Thomas had been his usual self but there had been a hard look in his eye which, for a moment, had reminded her of her late pa, Clem Cavendish. That look did not bode well for Irwin Kaye. The rancher would get his just deserts. Ignoring the curious glances and any questions about her brother's welfare and plans, Ivy headed home. Moss had indicated that he wished to pay his respects and she had accordingly invited him to Sunday tea. As yet Thomas was unaware that he would be sharing dinner with Moss. Given his present concerns she had not liked to tell him.

'Miz Tucker, is your brother going after Irwin Kaye?'

Ivy rounded on the questioner. 'How

would I know? I have more important things on my mind.'

Pole rubbed his long chin. There was not much in this town that Pole did not know. As telegraph clerk he was privy to a good deal of information. Cavendish did not rate highly in Pole's estimation. The sheriff had never been seen at Sunday service and it was known that Cavendish, although not frequenting the saloons, was not opposed to sharing a jug with Bart Parker.

Cavendish opened his office door and found Pole outside. Thinking the clerk had brought a telegram. Cavendish held out his hand. And then dropped it when it became clear Pole was not bearing a missive.

'What is it?' He stepped back and allowed Pole to enter the office. Concealing his dislike, Cavendish stared up into Pole's sallow face framed on either side by long greasy ginger hair.

'What is it?' Cavendish repeated.

'Are you going after Irwin Kaye,

Sheriff?' The words tumbled out eagerly.

'Are you offering to ride with me?' Cavendish snapped.

'Me? Well, no, er, I'm a family man, Sheriff.'

'So am I, in a manner of speaking.'

Pole looked down at the lawman. 'Sheriff,' he observed pompously, 'any other lawman would have saddled up and gone after Irwin Kaye long before now. It's lunchtime and — '

'And I'm eating my lunch.' Cavendish returned to his desk, assuming Pole would take the hint and vamoose.

'You were damn lucky last night, Sheriff.' Pole seemed inclined to talk and reluctant to leave.

'Luck had nothing to do with it. Now if you'll excuse me, Pole, I ain't of a mind to talk about luck.'

Pole ignored the blatant hint.

'It takes a brave man to go after Irwin Kaye.'

'Have you changed your mind about riding with me?' Cavendish demanded, his patience wearing thin.

'Certainly not. You can't expect me to involve myself in your feud with Irwin Kaye.'

'*My* feud, you say? Let me tell you I'm not feuding with Irwin Kaye. I'm a lawman and — '

'Naturally,' Pole interrupted and then winked. 'Naturally I don't blame you, Sheriff, for wanting to keep that woman to yourself, I'd do — '

Pole never got to say what he'd do for Cavendish, swiftly and unexpectedly and, more importantly, with accuracy, hurled his coffee pot at the telegraph clerk's head.

The pot struck the side of Pole's face. Steaming-hot coffee streamed down Pole's cheek. He screamed with pain and staggered out of the office clutching his face.

'I won't countenance that kind of talk. Don't you be forgetting yourself again, Pole,' Cavendish yelled.

'You're mad!' Pole howled, from the safety of the sidewalk. 'You've gone loco.'

'Well, I reckon you're showing your true colours, Sheriff.' Moss appeared in the doorway. His face, although now an unpleasant yellowish colour, was vastly improved from the last occasion Cavendish had seen him.

'Any objections?' Cavendish heard himself snarl.

'Me? No. I'm just a spectator.'

'Make yourself useful and brew up a replacement jug of coffee.' Cavendish sat down. As yet he did not know what his true colours might be. But he was changing, he conceded. Irwin Kaye and the apathy of Salt Creek were changing him.

* * *

Irwin Kaye's embossed wallpaper had been brought from the East at great expense. Now, heedless of that expense, Irwin Kaye hurled his coffee pot. Coffee ran in rivulets down the wall, ruining the paper.

Kaye had been expecting to reward

Eastman and Decker handsomely for a job well done. He had not anticipated his two men would be brought back to the Triple Crown lying stiff and cold in the back of a buck-board.

Patrick, who was with his pa, drew his .45 and with expertise twirled the weapon.

'The fact is,' he boasted, 'I've a hunch that today's going to be Cavendish's last day. What do you think, Pa? Let me deal with that little rat.'

Irwin poured himself a full whiskey. Unfortunately he did not have every confidence in Patrick. Thomas Cavendish was a proven killer. He had killed in Garland. Patrick was fast but maybe not fast enough to beat him. Cavendish had experience; all Patrick possessed was enthusiasm. Irwin sighed, instinct told him that this matter with Cavendish needed to be resolved and soon, because if it was not resolved and Patrick stepped in, he might lose Patrick. For the first time in his life Irwin experienced genuine fear.

'What do you say, Pa?' Patrick pressed.

'For now leave things to me,' Irwin ordered. 'We wait and see whether Cavendish comes to the Triple Crown. Have the men keep a look out. I want fair warning of his approach.' He grinned unpleasantly. 'And if he don't show, why I guess we've just got to pay him a visit!'

Kaye knew no one could get in or out of town without Preacher knowing about it. The old fanatic was afraid Cavendish might be persuaded to weaken and let the girl go free or else an attempt might be made to break her out. Preacher was determined the woman would hang. Kaye had no argument with that, nor did he want to argue with Preacher, at least not at the present time. What he needed was to persuade him to turn a blind eye should a chosen body of men ride into Salt Creek one dark night soon.

'Come on, Son, we'll pay a call on Preacher,' Kaye declared. He grinned.

'I've a hunch Cavendish won't come calling. If he tries to find men to ride with him, he won't find even one fool enough to tangle with the Triple Crown.'

'Why the hell have we got to see Preacher?' Patrick enquired.

'It's necessary,' Irwin stated. 'It's necessary to remind old Preacher that in times of drought he relies on Brocklehurst water to see him through. Well, now it's our water, Son, and Preacher can't take it for granted that we'll be inclined to be neighbourly.'

Irwin knew something none of the rest of Salt Creek knew. The railroad was coming through and it was Irwin's intention to buy up land and then sell at a high profit. There was a killing to be made in Salt Creek, and he was not only thinking of that little runt Sheriff Thomas Cavendish. He had thought to have Cavendish in his pocket, but now it was clear he was a treacherous varmint who'd take a man's money and then pull a double cross.

In the very same alleyway from which Eastman and Decker had sought to drygulch him, Thomas Cavendish stared across the darkened street. A light was visible from beyond the jailhouse shutters. Anyone passing might conclude Cavendish was 'at home'.

A dark shape scuttled past his boot. Cavendish believed that it would not only be four-legged rats out and about in Salt Creek tonight.

He squatted down, resting his back against solid wall. If they came for him tonight, as he believed they would, he thought they would hit hard and fast, escaping from town before Salt Creek's population realized what had happened.

Irwin Kaye would have to get past Preacher's guards. Cavendish was aware that in times of drought Preacher had been allowed to use Triple Crown water. Faced with such a choice, Preacher would doubtless consider Cavendish expendable. Steers would be a damn sight more important to Preacher than upholding the law.

Cavendish drifted into a state between sleep and consciousness with his thoughts dwelling pleasurably on Miss Irma.

The muffled sounds of hooves and a whinny brought him instantly awake, the thoughts of a naked Miss Irma banished. His back was stiff and aching and so was his rear, and he wondered he did not creak as he rose to his feet and peered cautiously out into the darkness, total darkness, for even the saloons had closed.

Dark shadows were gathered in front of the jail. The voices were muffled, but he did not need to hear what was being said, to know the intention of his enemies. He sniffed the breeze which carried the faint but distinguishable smell of kerosene. The skunks intended to fire his jail and in the process burn himself and his prisoner alive. To this end they were even barring his means of escape by placing brushwood against the jailhouse door.

Automatically his hand dropped to his .45 although he was confident no one would be able to spot him and he was content to be a mere spectator. Cavendish didn't give a damn whether Salt Creek's jail burnt, his days as sheriff were numbered. Eventually, the town, of necessity would be forced to construct a replacement.

Kerosene was sloshed with enthusiasm. Lights flared in the darkness as burning torches were applied to the tinder-dry kindling. Flames took hold immediately.

Irwin Kaye would be using his own men whom he had brought with him to Salt Creek. No doubt they had done things such as this before. Cavendish was not able to spot Kaye amongst the bunched men, which was too bad because he would have blasted Irwin there and then!

With whoops and victory yells, the assailants rode out. One paused and turned and to Cavendish's amazement held what appeared to be a bow and arrow. An arm drew back and the arrow sped on its way.

An almighty explosion shook Salt Creek. Cavendish reeled back. The bastards had sent a dynamite stick speeding towards the burning building.

Cavendish watched as the band thundered out of town. He guessed Kaye had paid a hefty fee for tonight's work and he found pleasure knowing that Kaye had wasted the blood money paid. He had achieved nothing.

Men and women, some in nightshirts and gowns, began to emerge, to mill around helplessly whilst voices yelled in excitement and disbelief.

Leaving them to it, seeing no reason at present to announce he was alive, Cavendish decided to return to his sister's home.

★　★　★

Whistling cheerfully, Moss headed for Ivy Tucker's home. Cavendish's demise was just the excuse needed for him to call and offer his condolences. Surely she'd need a shoulder to cry on?

Old Bart Parker had gotten drunk and had been heard loudly to declare that Salt Creek had lost a damn fine lawman. Significantly, no one save Bart had openly suggested that Irwin Kaye was responsible for the attack.

Miz Tucker answered the door. To his surprise Moss could not detect signs of grief upon her countenance.

'I've come to offer my condolences,' he blurted out, suddenly fearing a rebuff.

'Why, that is kind of you. Come in.' Ivy Tucker hurriedly closed the door behind him not wanting Moss to learn the truth too soon.

★ ★ ★

Studying his cigar smoke, Irwin Kaye allowed the members of the town council to prattle. Irwin had provided brandy, whiskey and cigars. They had met at his instigation. He even kept his lips buttoned while the fools praised the late sheriff and called him a fine upstanding man. He resisted the urge to clap when Sloan, a rancher of some standing, announced testily there was no need to get carried away, for after all the late Sheriff Cavendish had done nothing but sit on his butt or go fishing and . . .

'And what about that business in Garland?' Bart Parker interrupted angrily. Bart had joined the council members in the back room of the hotel; as the owner of the livery barn he was entitled to speak.

'As to the regrettable killings in Garland,' Sloan replied, 'Colonel Parker should have been lawfully arrested and put on trial for murder. Cavendish and Duffy showed themselves to be bullet-happy killers.'

'Shame on you!' Bart rejoined. 'And where were you, Irwin Kaye, when the sheriff was burnt inside his own jail?'

Preacher was surprisingly silent.

'And how is it, Preacher,' Bart Parker demanded, 'that these here so-called border raiders got past your lookouts unchallenged?' Surprisingly Bart was now sober having refused to touch Irwin's liquor.

'They'd been withdrawn,' Preacher muttered. 'I trusted Sheriff Cavendish to resist temptation,' he concluded lamely.

Patrick Kaye, who was also present, sniggered.

'So it is agreed then,' Irwin began, 'that Salt Creek needs a new lawman and that the late Sheriff Thomas Cavendish can be buried at the town's expense?'

'You haven't answered my question!' Bart challenged.

'I was at home at the Triple Crown. And so were my men. Anyone who says different is a goddamn liar.' He smiled. 'With the exception of Bart; I'll not argue with a man of his years.'

'Why you polecat . . . ' Bart spluttered.

'And my man Ellis can step into the void,' Irwin continued smugly. He paused. 'I take it no one here objects to Ellis?'

'Well, you take it wrong.' Cavendish stepped into the room. He'd been listening outside the door, biding his time. He smiled. 'I don't give a damn where you say you were, Mr Kaye. I'm still the Sheriff of Salt Creek. Whoever torched the jailhouse went to a whole lot of trouble for nothing. I ain't fool enough to allow myself to be burnt in my own jail.'

'But you allowed your prisoner to be burnt,' Sloan challenged nastily. 'A lawman who stands idle whilst his jail and prisoner burn is not fit to wear a star,' he continued self-righteously.

'Have you been drinking, Sloan?' Cavendish enquired.

'What the hell do you mean by that?' Sloan demanded.

'What do you mean by going out on a limb for Irwin Kaye?' Cavendish shrugged. 'Maybe he's paid you to stand in his corner.'

'You damn liar, Cavendish!'

'Quit yapping, Sloan. You're small fry.'

'I vote Cavendish be removed from office. He has proved his incompetence and inability to protect his prisoners so that the due process of law be observed.' Irwin Kaye glanced at the assembled men. 'Preacher!'

'I second that motion.' Preacher refused to meet Cavendish's eye.

Calmly Cavendish folded his arms. He smiled unpleasantly. 'So who's volunteering to remove me? Sure as hell I ain't about to resign. I've unfinished business to attend to.' He glared directly at Irwin leaving no one in doubt what that unfinished business might be.

Before his pa realized his intention, Patrick Kaye jumped right on in.

'That'll be my pleasure. You don't need to wait a moment more than is necessary, Shorty. I'll be more than happy to see you on your way. If you're man enough, follow me outside. It's pay-back time.'

'Patrick . . . ' Too late, Irwin realized events were spiralling out of his control.

'Stay out of this, Pa,' Patrick yelled. 'This is personal business between me and this two-timing little runt. This town ain't big enough for both of us and I ain't moving.'

Unexpectedly, Cavendish grinned. 'I've heard those words before. Seems to me I read those very same words in a dime novel.'

'If you're a yellow-belly, which I suspect you are, you can always shoot me in the back.' Patrick Kaye swaggered towards the door supremely confident that he could outgun Sheriff Thomas Cavendish, that no-account little bum who had tricked Pa into thinking he was one of the sheep.

'Your boy's loco, Mr Kaye. Why, even Jack McGinley would not turn his back upon a man he has just challenged,' a ranching man observed. 'But, by golly, your boy has guts. I'll say that for him, Irwin.'

Cavendish made no move to follow Patrick Kaye. He indicated the door. 'I'll follow along behind you, gentlemen. I'm not crazy enough to turn my back upon any one of you.'

'See here, Cavendish, we're not back-shooters.' Indignant protests ensued which Cavendish calmly ignored.

'Like I said, I'm not presenting my back as target. If you want to see gunplay, lead the way. If not, well, I am content to stay here as long as needs be.'

Still protesting, they began to move, as he had known they would, out through the door, out onto Main Street.

Irwin's control broke. He reached, not for the gun he wore strapped to his waist, but for the weapon he wore concealed in a shoulder holster . . .

5

Patrick Kaye stood in the middle of Main Street. Word had spread quickly that a gunfight was to take place and he was happy to be the centre of attention. He flexed his gunhand and grinned. It did not occur to him that he might lose.

On the middle finger of his gunhand he wore the distinctive silver ring he'd taken from the dead drifter's hand, a memento to remind him of his first successful gunfight. With pleasure he recalled the dead man's face, a stupid face with eyes which had bulged with terror. And that terror had served to increase Patrick's contempt.

Shots sounded from inside the hotel. For one long moment Patrick wondered what the hell was going on. Then suddenly he understood: his pa had robbed him of his moment of glory. He had shot Sheriff Thomas Cavendish.

Cursing obscenely, Patrick raced for the hotel intending to give his interfering pa hell. Nor did he care if the whole town heard what was said between father and son.

Two of his father's hired men followed him.

'Pa!' he yelled, as he burst into the room. But what confronted him was not his pa but Cavendish, smoking gun in hand, and that gun was pointing directly at Patrick's belly.

'You bastard!' Patrick confronted the pint-sized lawman.

Two events occurred simultaneously. To his disbelief, Patrick found himself shaking uncontrollably; he also found himself grabbed from behind and thrown to the ground.

'Don't shoot. For mercy's sake hold your fire Cavendish,' a familiar voice hollered.

Patrick recognized the voice. It belonged to Battle, a grizzled waddy, who had worked for Brocklehurst and who now worked for the Kayes.

'Goddamnit,' Tom Cavendish exclaimed, decidedly displeased. He'd been waiting his chance, waiting for Patrick to reach and when that happened Cavendish had intended to end things there and then. He was ready to kill Patrick Kaye.

'Goddamnit, Battle . . . '

'That's enough.' Sloan stepped between the lawman and Patrick Kaye. Battle and another man were having a hard time to hold Patrick down.

'I'll kill you, Cavendish. You . . . ' A string of obscenities followed. He threshed desperately. 'You're fired, Battle. Goddamn you.'

Cavendish kept an eye on Patrick Kaye. 'Don't worry Sloan, I won't blast him unless he draws first, which is mighty generous considering the Kayes tried to have me burnt alive. You all know it!'

No one spoke. And no one would meet his eye.

Cavendish holstered his gun. 'Hell!' he observed surlily 'There just ain't no pleasing some folk. And as for you,

Preacher, you ought to be damn well ashamed of yourself.'

To Cavendish's disbelief, Preacher sank to his knees. Fervently the old hypocrite began to pray for the soul of Irwin Kaye.

'For mercy's sake fetch the doc,' Battle was yelling. 'The boy has taken a fit.'

And so he had, Cavendish observed, as Patrick threshed around, spittle flecking his lips. Belatedly, a tablecloth was thrown over Irwin who had been temporarily overlooked in the light of new developments.

Cavendish regarded the assembled men. 'You won't be needing a new lawman.' No one disputed his remark. He had not been expecting them to. Allowing his gaze to first contemptuously sweep the townsmen, Cavendish strode out. Bart followed in his wake. Without speaking, the two headed for Bart's livery barn.

★   ★   ★

'Goddamnit, Doc! What do we do? Grief has driven him crazy.' Battle stared at the doc. He ignored Preacher. Battle, like Preacher, did not want to see Brocklehurst's spread go up for sale once again.

'Keep him away from Cavendish,' Doc advised. 'For the time being confine him to his room. Let him rant and rave. Give him a chance to work the hatred out of his system. Let him cool down. Pray that he sees sense.'

'Listen, boy!' Sloan shouted. 'The last thing you want to do is go after Cavendish. Just use your brains for a change. It's clear as day Cavendish tricked the both of you into challenging him publicly. Don't play into his hands.'

'If you ask me the Kayes have brought this misfortune upon themselves. As I recall, Salt Creek was an uneventful place until they came to town. I say the town ought to bill Patrick Kaye for a new jailhouse.' The speaker was Muller, a man who hitherto had shown little interest in the concerns of the town. 'And I don't reckon that the girl burned along with the jail,' Muller concluded. 'Cavendish ain't that kind of man. He would have gotten her out long before the jail was burnt.'

'She couldn't have gotten out of Salt Creek without my men spotting her,' Preacher rejoined.

'Then she's still in town,' Muller stated with certainty.

'Then I suggest you replace your guards,' Sloan snapped.

'Get Patrick home,' Adam Eden ordered. 'And if you don't want to see him dead, keep him under lock and key until he comes to his senses. From what I've seen, Patrick Kaye is not a match for Sheriff Cavendish.'

'Use your, brains, boy. Remember, brains.' Sloan gripped Patrick's shoulder. Sloan had his own reasons for wanting Sheriff Cavendish dead. What Muller had said made sense. Sloan suspected Cavendish wanted the woman outlaw, and knowing Cavendish he would not want to see the woman hang. She had to hang and this was not because justice must be done. Sloan didn't give a damn about justice, although in this case no one could argue she was not an out-and-out widelooper.

'You get him out of here, Battle.' Moss stood in the doorway. 'Now!'

'You bet.' Battle was quick to obey the ex-ramrod.

'Mr Sloan, I don't reckon you know what you're saying.' Sloan and Moss locked eyes. Surprisingly, Sloan was the first to break the gaze.

Eden recognized that there was more to Moss's words than was apparent, but he could not work out what that extra meaning might be.

Moss had been taking tea when one of Ivy's girls had burst in with news concerning the events at the meeting. That Ivy Tucker had deceived him had given Moss something to think about.

'Where's Cavendish?' Moss enquired sourly.

'Well, if he ain't gone home I reckon

he'll be with Bart Parker,' Muller volunteered. He shrugged. 'And that's where I'm heading. Home. And I'm staying at my ranch until this trouble has blown over. This ain't my fight. I don't give a damn about Cavendish and the Kayes. And as for the woman, well, if she was a man I'd say she had to hang but a woman well, hell . . . '

Moss watched as Patrick Kaye was removed, twitching and yelling. Irwin was left where he lay. Moss frowned; Miz Tucker would have the job of laying Irwin out. He guessed it would not bother her. She was Clem Cavendish's daughter after all. The late Clem Cavendish had been a ruthless killer, but even Clem could not be compared to Brain.

Moss was pretty sure Sloan had heard of Mark Brain. And maybe the name would be familiar to Patrick Kaye.

From time to time, Moss still awoke drenched with sweat. Every now and then his nightmares returned. He'd lie in the darkness haunted by the smiling features of Mark Brain.

Mark Brain had been Moss's childhood friend. In the opinion of those who knew about him, he was an evil monster and madman.

At the beginning of the nightmare, Mark Brain's face was a nothingness, a round circle about the size of a thumbnail, but that face moved slowly towards him all the while growing in size until it filled Moss's vision. Blood dripped from his teeth, blood and unthinkable, unmentionable substances.

In his mind, Moss heard again Brain's high-pitched chilling laughter. 'I've done it,' he had shouted. 'I've done what Teacher told me and got myself some brains.'

Whenever Moss had tried to absolve himself from guilt he'd always told himself that Teacher White had not been blameless. The old idiot had brought misfortune upon himself. Taking a dislike to the slow Mark Brain,

White had made Mark's life a misery, hitting the luckless scholar every chance he got declaring that he believed in beating brains into obstinate boys. Little had he known that he was igniting a stick of dynamite and when it had gone up, old White had paid a high price for his petty cruelty.

When Moss had found Mark Brain together with the remains of White, Mark having ignited, had, in Moss's words, burnt himself to a frizzle, it would have been easy indeed to take Mark to the sheriff.

Young Joe Moss, however, had gone home, gotten himself a shovel and together the two had buried what was left of the teacher. They'd buried the remains deep and concealed the evidence of digging.

'You've got to go,' Moss had said. 'In case!' he'd added. He'd known that Mark, being a decent sort, would not have tried to blame a friend for the crime. Moss was not worried about himself; Mark would never have mentioned Joe's involvement.

'In case they find out,' Mark had muttered, and so, scared to the tips of his worn boots, Mark Brain had quit their home town.

Eighteen months later, following the death of his ailing ma, Moss himself had quit, taking care not to head in the same direction as Mark.

After burying White's remains, young Moss had taken to rolling himself smokes. Now Moss rolled himself another smoke. To have heard Sloan shouting about brains had been one almighty shock. Moss didn't like to think he'd once been pals with Mark Brain.

Moss prayed that Patrick Kaye had not heard of Mark Brain.

★ ★ ★

'You could let the girl go,' Bart Parker suggested. 'I'll saddle up two horses. Escort her out of town. Just tell 'em she eluded you in the confusion of the burning.'

'Don't think I haven't thought of that.' Cavendish raised Bart's jug to his lips and took a swallow. 'The fact is, Bart, it's not likely Preacher called off his guards. I guess he just instructed them to turn a blind eye and not to challenge any supposed border raiders riding into town or riding out. Preacher has a long knife out for Miss Irma. I'm damned if I can figure it out. True she's a widelooper, there's more to this than meets the eye.'

'Talk of the devil! He's tracked you down. Here he comes and it won't be to apologize for letting Kaye's men get to you.'

Bart was right. 'An eye for an eye,' Preacher declared emphatically without preamble. Spittle flecked his lips and there was a glint in his eye which boded ill. Cavendish held his peace and allowed Preacher to continue. 'That female is going to hang.' Preacher snorted contemptuously. 'Satan is a woman,' he continued, warming to the subject. 'You've been tested, Cavendish, and found wanting.'

Cavendish stifled a grin. 'Make up your mind, you crazy old coot. One moment I'm trustworthy and guards are not needed and the next I've been found wanting. I reckon you're wanting as well, Preacher. Wanting in the head.' He smiled slightly. He could have said that he had been tested and Miss Irma had not found him wanting. Last night she'd surprised him by showing her gratitude.

'I'm counting on you to see me free, Cavendish,' she'd said.

'You ain't going to hang, Irma,' he'd vowed.

'I'm not jesting, Sheriff,' Preacher stated grimly.

Cavendish thinned his lips. So Preacher had figured out Irma was still around. The old devil was determined upon a hanging.

'You never did call off your guards,' Cavendish essayed.

Preacher remained mute. The silence was answer enough.

'I'm not jesting,' Cavendish rejoined grimly. 'And I'm telling you now, that woman ain't going to hang. Don't cross me, Preacher.'

'What the hell do you mean?' Preacher demanded angrily. 'She's as guilty as sin and I ain't just referring to rustling steers.'

'She ain't going to hang and that's all I've got to say on the matter. Now leave me in peace, Preacher.'

'You ain't heard the last of this,' Preacher yelled, determined on the last word. 'You're besotted, Tom Cavendish. I'm going to pray you come to your senses before it is too late.' So saying Preacher stalked away.

'There ain't many like Preacher,' Bart observed. He wiped his lips, 'Thank the Lord. Preacher is clearly a woman-hater.'

'He seems to hate Miss Irma,' Cavendish agreed, thinking that if Irwin Kaye could railroad this town, he could also. He could railroad this town into finding Miss Irma innocent. In that event she would have every right to ride out and if anyone tried to stop her, well, Cavendish knew what he'd do. Word would soon spread that Sheriff Cavendish wished to see Miss Irma acquitted.

Events were getting out of hand, but as the late Clem Cavendish would have said there was no turning back the clock.

★ ★ ★

For a time, Patrick Kaye was as a man demented. Repeatedly he struck his head against the wall of his room unable to face the truth, that his father was dead and that Cavendish was strutting around Salt Creek.

Outside the locked door, Battle yelled unwanted advice.

'Calm yourself, boss. Face facts. You're in no state to go after Thomas Cavendish. You need a calm mind and a steady hand and sure as hell, you ain't got a calm mind.'

Patrick cussed Battle profoundly and told him he was sacked.

'What good will it do getting yourself killed?' Battle questioned. 'Use your brains like Mr Sloan said.'

Battle didn't give a damn whether the young varmint got himself planted six feet under. Battle's concern was the future of the ranch and the future of his own job. With young Kaye dead, the ranch would go up for sale again. It was a thankless task nursemaiding the young varmint. Battle knew the Kayes were behind the attack on the jail, but Sheriff Cavendish hadn't forced the Kayes into confrontation. They'd done that themselves, forced the confrontation and paid the price.

Finally Patrick Kaye fell silent. 'Boss', Battle had called him boss. The word registered. It was all his now, this huge ranch, the bank balance, the crew and all the power that went along with being the boss of the Triple Crown ranch.

And then Patrick remembered!

Pa had been joking one day, joking with Moss.

'Hell,' Pa had said, 'if that little runt gives me any trouble I ought to send for Mark Brain.'

'How'd you hear about Mark Brain?' Moss had not been laughing.

'Sloan was saying something.' Pa had related what Sloan had said concerning Mark Brain. 'Is it true?' Irwin had asked Moss.

'How do I know?' Moss had rejoined. He shrugged. 'Hell boss, Sloan was yarning you.'

But Sloan, Patrick decided, did not yarn. And he seemed to remember Sloan shouting at him to use his brain.

'Use your brain, boss,' Battle yelled. 'McGinley is coming to town. Let him take care of Cavendish.'

Pa hadn't paid McGinley to take care of Cavendish. And neither had anyone else. Whatever the town might believe, Patrick knew McGinley; whatever his reasons for heading this way, if indeed he was heading for Salt Creek, taking care of Sheriff Thomas Cavendish was not one of them.

Patrick sat silent. His first job was to persuade that darn fool Battle to let him out. Battle was on borrowed time. As soon as was practicable Patrick aimed to fire him.

★ ★ ★

Idly, Cavendish wondered how his sister and Moss had gotten on down at Salt Creek. She'd certainly returned home looking pleased with herself. But what in tarnation were her intentions? Moss was sniffing round and Cavendish guessed when McGinley hit town Miz Tucker would have McGinley sniffing round also.

Hell, Cavendish decided he did not wish to know his sister's intention.

★ ★ ★

On the way back from their picnic at Salt Creek, Moss had found himself telling Ivy Tucker about Mark Brain.

They'd met Battle on their way back from Salt Creek and Battle had been inclined to talk.

'That young fool has headed for the Badlands,' Battle had informed Moss gloomily. 'He's given me the slip and left word that he's going to look for some *hombre* called Mark Brain. I ain't never heard of him.'

'See you around, Battle.' Moss had speeded up the buggy so much that Miz Tucker had demanded to know what was so special about Mark Brain.

And Moss had found himself confiding the truth about certain habits Mark Brain had acquired. It was a relief to be able to talk and Ivy had been interested rather than affronted.

'And he has a habit,' Moss had heard himself say, 'leastways upon occasion when the mood takes him, of splitting them open, the heads that is, taking out the brains and eating them. Fried or boiled,' Moss had concluded.

'Well, leastways, he don't eat them

raw,' Ivy had rejoined. 'You know you'll have to tell Thomas. All of this. Even though you say Mark Brain would never come to Salt Creek in a million years.'

'I truly believe it,' Moss had declared. 'Mark ain't no hired killer like some I could mention. He only turns on those who have done him wrong.'

'Some you could mention?' She had essayed.

'Jack McGinley is coming to town. And I've heard tell it was you who sent for him. What are your intentions, ma'am?' Considering what had taken place at Salt Creek, Moss considered he had a right to know. His ears grew a brilliant red as he remembered the goings-on.

'My intentions! How dare you question me, Joseph Moss. You can leave this buggy and proceed on foot. And be sure to tell Thomas what you know.'

So saying, Ivy Tucker had driven away leaving Moss to stare after her.

Miz Tucker, he reflected, had a cast-iron stomach. Mark Brain's habits had not disturbed her constitution in the least. And when Moss had recounted his nightmares she'd merely advised him to think of sheep.

Scratching his head, Moss set out to find Sheriff Thomas Cavendish, not that he expected the diminutive lawman to show gratitude upon being fore-warned of possible danger.

Moss had heard talk in the saloons. That is, he'd heard one of the saloon women, in particular, giving her consid-ered opinion.

'You men are fools,' the woman had joked. 'It's plain as the nose on your face how to get rid of Cavendish. When this female law-breaker leaves Salt Creek she won't leave solo. Hell, if Tom Cavendish does but know it he doesn't need to make threats to achieve his objective.'

The bartender had nodded. 'It makes sense. If that woman is found guilty Cavendish might really go loco and start blasting folk for the fun of it.'

Dyers, the owner of the Golden Garter, had nodded his agreement.

'Set the girl free and there won't be a problem,' the saloon woman had advised. She smiled. 'I must admit I'm kind of curious about the sheriff. He ain't the man we thought him to be . . .'

Well, that was a fact, Moss agreed as he headed for the livery barn which now served as a temporary sheriff's office. Cavendish had made himself more unpopular than ever by issuing numerous unspecific threats regarding the outcome of Irma's trial. Folk in Salt Creek didn't want a lawman who threw his weight around.

And everyone knew Tom Cavendish's days of fishing and snoozing were over.

Moss found himself wondering whether Cavendish knew what Miz Tucker's intentions concerning Jack McGinley might be.

6

Something was wrong and Cavendish had no idea what it was. He only knew that he felt decidedly uneasy. Everyone in town seemed readily to agree that Irma should be found innocent. No one was arguing. The exception, of course, was Preacher. But then Cavendish had not expected that old leopard to change his spots.

Cavendish therefore concluded that perhaps the town intended to double-cross him, first allowing him to believe they'd find Irma innocent and then declaring her guilty.

He clenched his jaw. If that were the case the jury and town would pay dearly. His sister was suggesting that perhaps folk had seen enough trouble and did not want more. Cavendish remained unconvinced.

Halfway down Main Street, Cavendish

spotted Bart sitting by the window of the town's best restaurant.

At certain times Salt Creek stank, sanitation not being what it ought and this was one such time. Undeterred, Cavendish joined Bart at the restaurant table.

'It's on the house, Sheriff.' The proprietor, aptly named Slim Jim, greeted Cavendish affably, which in itself heightened Cavendish's suspicions.

'I pay my way,' Cavendish declared sourly. Jim chuckled. 'Come now, Sheriff, a free meal can't rightly be taken as a bribe.'

'He accepts,' Bart declared, 'and if he don't, I'll order and eat for both of us.'

'Fine by me,' Jim rejoined.

Sitting down, Cavendish stared out while Bart proceeded to order with enthusiasm. Three dust-stained riders made their way down Main Street. Momentarily Cavendish gave them his attention. They were clearly heading for one of the saloons.

'Saddle tramps!' Bart snorted. 'Times are hard.'

'They sure are.' Jim seemed inclined to linger. 'You'd think a man with a fair-size spread to run would stay put. A man with brains wouldn't go haring off on mysterious business, business he seems loath to divulge, but which might concern your good self, Sheriff Cavendish!'

'Let me worry about Patrick Kaye.' Cavendish gave Jim his attention, the saddle tramps forgotten. He wondered how much Jim knew. Mark Brain beggared belief.

'He ain't totally bad,' Moss had concluded lamely.

'Just mad!' Cavendish had observed drily. 'But as long as he stays in the Badlands, your pal Mark Brain ain't my concern. And I'm betting Patrick Kaye will never make it across, in any event. That young varmint ain't got what it takes.'

'I'll agree on that,' Moss had said, and had then astounded Cavendish by enquiring whether he knew Miz Tucker's intentions concerning McGinley.

'They were at school together. So you could say they go way back. Beyond that I cannot say. My sister's intentions are her own concern.' Cavendish had paused. 'How did you like your picnic at Salt Creek?' he had concluded innocently. That had done the trick, Moss had rapidly made himself scarce.

Cavendish stared at the steak Jim's hired woman had placed before him. He shook his head. 'Nope,' he drawled, 'I ain't hungry at all.' Thinking of Mark Brain had turned his stomach.

'That's mighty generous of you, Sheriff.' Bart shovelled Cavendish's meat on to his own plate.

Absent-mindedly, Cavendish watched as Bart voraciously shovelled food as if afraid Jim would whip the plate away.

Cavendish concluded that Moss had not completely turned against his one-time friend, albeit that friend had become a monster.

'What's your plan?' Bart questioned

unexpectedly. He grinned. 'You ain't got one, other than blasting Preacher if he crosses you. You'd best have a care, Tom, or you'll find yourself on the wrong side of the law.'

Jim's hired woman directed her broom at the scuffed toe of Cavendish's boot.

'What in tarnation has got into you woman?' Bart demanded diverted from his steak.

'Why, Sheriff Cavendish ain't no better than Patrick Kaye!' she declared, planting her hands on ample hips as she glared at Cavendish.

'Now what are you talking about woman?' Bart spoke on Cavendish's behalf.

'What's he been doing to that poor helpless creature he's got hidden away . . .'

'You ain't referring to Miss Irma, are you, ma'am?' Cavendish rubbed his chin. 'I can assure you she ain't a helpless creature.'

'So you say.'

'Ask her yourself,' Cavendish shrugged. 'Just go on over to Miz Tucker's place and satisfy your curiosity.'

'Well, I . . . ' Flustered she dropped her gaze. 'Maybe I'm misjudging you,' she concluded lamely.

'I reckon a good many folk have misjudged Sheriff Cavendish,' Bart declared.

'The ranchers ain't with you Sheriff,' Slim Jim announced abruptly. He shrugged. 'I hear talk that's all.'

'What kind of talk?' Bart asked eagerly, before Cavendish could get a word in.

'Seems like Sloan is siding with Preacher,' Jim advised. 'Sloan reckons a woman should be treated the same as a man.'

'But only when it's a hanging matter,' Cavendish observed drily.

'And the ranchers tend to agree with Sloan,' Jim continued. 'The town may be in your pocket, but outside town boundaries that's another matter. What are you gonna do, Sheriff? You can't blast the whole damn bunch. No way will that woman ride free.'

'I aim to stand my ground,' Cavendish replied simply. He was prepared to die to save Irma. Much depended upon whether his opponents were prepared to die to get their way. He guessed not.

Lawmen had done worse than see a guilty prisoner set free and got away with it.

'There's some say you ain't fit to be a lawman, Sheriff!' Slim Jim observed maliciously as Bart shovelled in the last mouthful of food. Grease trickled down his stubbly chin. 'Hell, Bart, you're beginning to look like a saddle bum yourself,' Jim joked, temporarily diverted from Cavendish.

'What the hell,' Cavendish exclaimed rising to his feet.

The woman stood in the middle of Main Street. Blood stained the front of her yellow silk gown and as Cavendish stepped from the restaurant he observed that blood also smeared her cheeks. It was not her own blood he decided.

'It's Dyers!' she screeched before Cavendish could speak. 'He's taken a beating. And Maggie! The bastard has beaten Maggie real bad!'

Cavendish guessed he knew who she was talking about. It had to be the three strangers. They were big men. The kind he would have to look up to. They would think him a joke. His star would mean nothing to them.

So he had one almighty problem. The chances of him being able to resolve this matter peaceably were nil. And leaving enemies around to try and kill him another day was a fatal mistake.

'How bad?' Cavendish queried, as he headed towards the saloon.

'No one can get in to see but we heard her screaming. She's quiet now. Dyers was on his way up when one of them clubbed him down from behind.' The woman stifled a sob. 'And kicked him real bad!'

Cavendish halted abruptly. Coming towards him was the last person he expected to see. Wheels began to turn. Sure as hell Sloan was up to something. The woman tugged at his sleeve but Cavendish ignored her. What did Sloan want? That question was easy to answer: Sloan wanted Sheriff Tom Cavendish out of the way; Sloan wanted Irma to hang. No doubt Sloan thought Sheriff Tom Cavendish a simple-minded fool.

'They don't want trouble, Sheriff!' Sloan's words confirmed Cavendish's suspicions.

Cavendish confronted the rancher. Sloan's face was flushed. 'Where do you fit into this?' Cavendish enquired.

'There's no need for bloodshed. Let them take their companion and ride out.'

'They've beaten Maggie real bad and — '

Sloan ignored the woman. 'Take it easy, Sheriff. It won't be the first time men too long on the trail have gotten out of hand.'

'I guess not.' Cavendish was prepared

to play along for now.

'Let's go on over the saloon and sort this out,' Sloan suggested. 'I'll lead the way.'

'You don't give a damn,' the woman screeched. She lunged at Cavendish, but Bart, who'd caught up with Cavendish stuck out a foot and tripped her.

'Give me a hand,' Bart hollered.

'Goddamnit!' Cavendish exclaimed, as he observed Bart tustling with the crazed woman. Bart, in Cavendish's opinion, was exhibiting a mite too much enthusiasm.

'Lead the way, Sloan,' he ordered, tearing his eyes away from a thrashing leg and black silk stocking. Sloan also was looking.

'It's not as if a decent woman has been assaulted.' Sloan led the way towards the saloon. 'And you no longer have a jail do you, Sheriff?' There was a note in Sloan's voice which made Cavendish's hackles rise.

'That is a consideration,' Cavendish

agreed. And so it was but not in the way Sloan might imagine. 'So I'm not at risk you'd say,' he queried mildly.

'Not at all. Not if you act reasonably,' Sloan was quick to reassure him.

'I'm a reasonable man, Sloan,' Cavendish rejoined. He paused. 'But I never knew you was an altruistic man!'

'Trust me, Sheriff! I've reasoned with them.'

Cavendish nodded. Behind him the woman screamed obscenities but Bart and Jim had a hold on her.

Cavendish halted before the saloon. Irma was the thought uppermost in his mind. She was depending upon him to save her neck. If he died, Salt Creek would renege. She'd be found guilty and they'd hang her for sure.

'You go on in, Sloan.' Cavendish smiled. 'I trust you to pave the way. I won't be arresting anyone for assaulting Dyers and Maggie.' That was for sure given the kind of *hombres* he'd be dealing with. 'I'll be coming in gun holstered and ready to talk,' he lied, unable to believe he could fool Sloan so easily.

Sloan nodded.

'I expect them to holster their weapons.'

'I'll see to it!' Sloan disappeared through the bat-wings.

Cavendish knew there was no reasoning with a drunk. He wasn't fool enough to try. Sloan unknowingly had played into Cavendish's hands. Whilst they had been talking he had put together a plan of sorts.

When he had first patrolled Salt Creek, Cavendish had chanced upon Pastor Michaels hot-footing it up the stairs which led up to the top floor of Dyers' establishment. These stairs were conveniently sited in a narrow alleyway. Cavendish had thought no more of it until now. He'd seen the pastor's wife and understood why the man sought more amenable companionship.

Stepping into the alleyway, Cavendish moved cautiously up the stairs gun in hand. His problems would start if

Dyers had seen fit to bar the door. Cavendish's hand closed over the door handle and, to his relief, the door opened without even a creak. Clearly Dyers kept the hinges well oiled. Gun drawn, he stepped into the saloon and moved silently down the corridor.

Maggie's room would be along this corridor. Cavendish was familiar with the set-up of the saloon, not that he had ever availed himself of these particular facilities. As all the doors were shut, presumably Maggie was still shut in with the man who had assailed her. Before he could even begin to help Maggie he must deal with the two men below at the bar, the two who had felled Dyers and were now waiting to deal with Salt Creek's sheriff.

'You get him in here. Tell him we don't want trouble. We just want to leave peaceable. That's reasonable, ain't it?'

Cavendish looked down on the scene below. The two men faced the batwings. Both held Colt .45s drawn and pointed.

Customers, Cavendish saw, had been herded out of the way leaving the two with a clear shot at whoever came through the batwings.

'What the hell are we gonna do, Mitch?'

'A bullet to the knee will slow him some.' Mitch laughed, 'You're right, Sloan. We don't want to kill no lawman.'

'Call him in,' Mitch's companion ordered.

'Come on in, Sheriff. It's safe,' Sloan called out carefully moving himself out of the line of fire.

Cavendish thinned his lips. It was as he had known it would be. The pair below were gunning for him, maybe not to kill him outright, for killing a lawman could stir up a hornets' nest, but they sure as hell intended leaving him crippled and useless.

Dyers lay on the floor groaning softly. It was then Sloan lifted his head. He looked upwards straight into Cavendish's face. As Sloan's face registered disbelief, Cavendish's instinct for self-preservation took over and his finger squeezed the trigger. He knew instantly there was no other way, for already Sloan's mouth was opening to shout a warning. He was going to warn the two bums!

Cavendish's first bullet struck Mitch, back of the head, his second hit Mitch's companion mid-forehead, for the man was turning, gun raised to shoot.

A woman screamed. It was not a pleasant sight. Doors were opening along the corridor. Men in various states of undress emerged with the women they'd been with, hovering uncertainly in the background. One door remained shut. Cavendish knew it had to belong to Maggie. Without hesitation angling his .45 he blasted the lock.

'Goddamnit!' he yelled, suffused with anger as his eyes took in the sight which greeted him. Maggie's customer was passed out cold. He lay on top of Maggie and as for Maggie herself,

Cavendish saw that she was semi-conscious. Blood covered what he could see of her face and hair.

Cavendish seized the drunk by the long single pigtail of greasy hair and hauled the man off the prone woman.

People flooded into the room, foremost amongst them Bart and the woman who had raised the alarm.

'You dealt with them fine, Sheriff!' she declared.

'Couldn't have done a better job myself,' Bart agreed.

'Good Lord, man, you shot two men about to surrender.'

Cavendish spun round angrily. 'Do you take me for a fool, Sloan? Surrender, my foot. At the least they would have left me a cripple. You set me up. Now get out of my sight before I forget I'm a lawman. And one of you get Doc, this girl needs help real bad.' He met the woman's eye. 'Maggie might never be right in the head again,' he warned. 'Best steel yourself.'

She nodded. 'It's one of the risks of

the profession. What do you aim to do about that varmint?' She kicked the man with her bright red shoe as she spoke. He grunted but did not come round.

'Well, as to that, we'll keep him cuffed and locked up here,' Cavendish decreed. 'Judge Gough will be here shortly; he can try this bastard before he gets round to trying Miss Irma.'

'Hell, Sheriff, the most he'll get is a fine. Ain't no jury in this town is going to find him guilty,' the woman argued.

'That's true, Thomas.' Ivy Tucker had arrived. 'You'd best get your cuffs and leg irons. And get these folk out of here.' She paused. 'Get a rider out to the Brady place. Doc's out there tending Mrs Brady. She's due any time.' She gripped her brother's arm. 'You may have trouble finding the leg irons but they're around.'

'Get out of here.' Cavendish shepherded folk out of the room. His sister had had a peculiar glint in her eye which had reminded Thomas of the late

Clem Cavendish.

'You ain't fit to raise those young ones, Clem Cavendish!' The minister's wife hadn't been afraid to speak her mind. Clem hadn't uttered a word to contradict her.

'Ain't no arguing with a determined woman,' he'd said later. Shortly afterwards, Clem had taken Tom and Ivy and left town.

'First time I've been run out of town,' he joshed, 'and by a woman.'

Cavendish had a hunch that the man who'd pulped Maggie's head would not get to see Judge Gough after all.

★   ★   ★

Patrick Kaye rode south. As much as he missed his pa, being the undisputed boss of the Triple Crown Ranch more than compensated for his loss. He was the one giving the orders and it made him feel good.

He'd feel even better watching

Cavendish suffer. Patrick planned to watch as Mark Brain did his worst.

★ ★ ★

The stage carrying Judge Gough and Jack McGinley bowled into Salt Creek. McGinley had noticed, even if the judge had not, that the trail into Salt Creek was being watched.

McGinley's first sight of Salt Creek was the town's cemetery. As the stage bowled past it slowed giving McGinley a chance to observe the three freshly dug graves and the small crowd which had gathered to hear the ranting preacher. McGinley heard the name Cavendish mentioned. He smiled slightly, thinking it looked as though Cavendish was responsible for the graves and whatever else was going on in this town. Sure as hell this town had been stirred. McGinley knew and recognized the signs.

'The jail has been burnt!' Mrs Gough exclaimed.

'So it has, ma'am,' McGinley agreed. 'Maybe you've been cheated out of a hanging, Judge,' he taunted softly.

Judge Gough made no response. He had been unusually quiet throughout the journey. McGinley knew why. Twenty years back Judge Gough had hired McGinley to do away with Reginald's brother, Reginald's rival for the hand of the now Mrs Reginald Gough. That a stampede had done the job before McGinley could get round to it did not signify. Money had changed hands. And in McGinley's opinion that made Judge Reginald Gough no better than the luckless folk Judge Gough sentenced to hang.

The sight of the ruined jail cheered Judge Gough. If the woman had died in the fire there would be no trial. He could take the next stage out. He could get away from McGinley. He did not care for the way his wife and daughter blushed when McGinley spoke to either of them. Both had professed themselves shocked by McGinley's calling and

Judge Gough refused to believe for one minute . . .

McGinley frowned slightly, the thought occurring to him that with the jail burnt, Gough had an excuse to leave. McGinley knew the signs. The women were interested. It was his reputation which had initially aroused them he knew. Reputations could be useful!

McGinley grinned, even with a reputation Sheriff Thomas Cavendish wasn't likely to find attractive women interested in becoming better acquainted. Especially not two fine women like these ones.

'Allow me, ma'am.' McGinley was quick to disembark for it gave him a chance to get his hands around two trim waists. He was confident that Judge Reginald wouldn't do a damn thing about it.

McGinley found himself wondering whether he'd get a chance to get his hands around Ivy Tucker's somewhat broader waist.

7

Cavendish stood outside Doc's place. He'd been to check up on Maggie. It didn't look good. Across Main Street, passengers were alighting from the stage. He recognized McGinley and Judge Gough. The two women were strangers but evidently with Gough.

Sloan and Eden, Cavendish observed, had taken it upon themselves to meet the stage. Cavendish was puzzled as to why these two had stepped into the picture. He had no quarrel with either Sloan or Eden. All along he had thought Irwin Kaye would be his number-one problem. Well, he guessed he was wrong. Sloan was proving to be a conniving skunk. And Cavendish knew Sloan was working to turn the town against him.

All Cavendish had done had been to uphold the law. And if he wished to express an opinion concerning Irma's trial he had every right to do so. That certain folk were getting het up about the deaths at the saloon was a puzzle.

'Trust a lawman not to be around when he's needed,' Dyers had complained. Right now Dyers was laid up with broken ribs, but Dyers still had his faculties which was more than could be said for the unfortunate Maggie.

'I ain't a fortune teller,' Cavendish had defended himself.

'Are you not?' There had been an odd expression on Dyer's countenance. But Dyers had not commented further. They both knew to what Dyers had been referring.

Commotion had broken out in the saloon when one of the girls had ran screeching down the stairs. Maggie's attacker, it seemed, had drowned himself.

'Got himself into the tub and drowned!' the girl had screamed repeatedly.

'Well, I guess I won't be needing these.' Cavendish had put the leg irons and cuffs to one side.

Commotion had broken out again behind him as he'd walked out.

'Damn it, man, ain't you going to investigate?' the barber had indignantly exclaimed.

'How could an insensible man get himself into a tub of water?' Eden had demanded. 'I demand you do your job, Sheriff!'

Folk, Cavendish reflected, saw what they wanted to see, and the folk of Salt Creek apparently saw a sheriff who wasn't fulfilling his duties. Cavendish, on the other hand, saw himself as a victim of circumstances beyond his control. But certain folk were saying he had brought his problems upon himself. Preacher, although not openly, was accusing him of being a renegade lawman. So were Eden and Sloan.

Cavendish smiled drily. Yep, he reflected, folk saw what they wanted. Take George, the stage driver, for instance. Folk saw a hard-drinking and hard-cussing man of indeterminable years, a man who would not again be sober until it was time to take the next stage out, but Cavendish had seen from the first there was something about George which did not set right.

George's secret was safe. No way was Cavendish minded to accuse George of being a woman. George could keep her secret until she dropped dead, then the truth would out. But Cavendish would not be around Salt Creek to witness the disclosure. He was through with this town. It was time to move on. Irma had been talking of Canada, and making it clear Cavendish was welcome to travel along with her.

Cavendish scowled. Preacher was heading his way. He had joined Sloan and Eden and spoken with Gough. Eden and Sloan, their business concluded, were heading in a different direction.

Preacher reminded Cavendish of a dog with its teeth into a juicy bone. The old lunatic could not let the matter of Irma's hanging rest. Carefully, Cavendish began to roll himself a smoke. So doing kept his hands busy. Right now his hands itched to squeeze Preacher's scrawny neck.

'I didn't think you'd have stomach to greet the stage,' Preacher stated without preamble. 'Doubtless you're finding it hard to look Judge Gough in the eye.'

Cavendish shrugged. Such nonsense did not deserve a response.

'Which is understandable seeing as you're trying to prevent justice from taking its course,' Preacher continued. 'One of my crew was killed. Young Newman. For all we know that woman could have fired the bullet which took an innocent life.'

Again Cavendish shrugged.

'Well, Sheriff, you'll see the scaffolding going up pretty damn soon. Judge Gough is willing to try the case as soon as the scaffolding is up. There's no wriggling out of it, Sheriff. You'd best be ready to produce your prisoner.'

'Get out of my sight, you old hypocrite!'

Preacher swallowed. 'You're a lawman.

If you don't care to uphold the law maybe you should hand over to someone who does.'

'My head's pounding, Preacher. If you don't oblige me by leaving, you'll suffer the indignity of being thrown off the sidewalk,' Cavendish threatened.

'And you'd do it. That woman has got to you, Cavendish. Justice means nothing to you now. But justice will be done. Just you wait and see!'

Rapidly, Preacher backed away as Cavendish took a step towards him.

'Packed his first wife off to the asylum, so I've heard tell.' Doc joined Cavendish upon the sidewalk. Judge Gough was heading for the hotel. McGinley had seen the ladies into the hotel some time ago.

'What about the second?' Cavendish asked idly.

'In my opinion, the woman would have come right in time. She'd lost a baby and had taken to talking to herself and weeping chronic.' Doc paused. 'But I wasn't around in those

141

days. Preacher had his way: he got rid of her.'

'That sounds like Preacher,' Cavendish observed.

'And his second wife ran off. Disappeared without trace,' Doc added with relish. 'Now she couldn't be blamed for that, seeing as she was a young woman and he was long in the tooth even then.'

'Did you know her, Doc?'

Doc shook his head. 'As I've said this was before my time.'

'You don't like him do you, Doc?'

'No.'

Cavendish smiled maliciously. 'Maybe she's still alive, the first wife that is. Do folk ever come out? Sure as hell it would be a surprise for Preacher, wouldn't you say?'

'What are you saying?'

'I'm saying I'd like to see Preacher squirm. My pa always believed in paying folk back. Well, Preacher has brought out the worst in me, Doc. Short of strangling or shooting him you tell me a better way.'

'You've given me one hell of an idea, Sheriff!'

'I won't ask what that idea might be,' Cavendish rejoined. His eyes narrowed. 'Come to think of it, Doc, you've given *me* one hell of an idea.'

'And what might that be?'

Cavendish lowered his voice.

Doc shook his head. 'That can't be, Cavendish. You're grasping at straws.'

'That ain't the point, Doc. It don't have to be true. I ain't seeking the truth, just a legitimate reason for keeping that old coot out of my hair.'

Doc hooted with laughter. 'You're loco, Cavendish. And you ain't got that much hair!'

'So I've been told.' Cavendish grinned. 'You've made my day, Doc.'

'Where do you plan to stow him?' Doc enquired. He winked. 'I'd best know just in case you forget that he's been stowed away.'

Cavendish shook his head. 'I wouldn't do that, Doc. I just want

Preacher out of the way. I don't particularly want him dead. Unnecessary killing ain't my way.' He paused, Doc didn't look entirely convinced. 'Kent's well. I noted it's boarded and dry,' Cavendish concluded.

Doc nodded. 'I dare say he'll be accommodated far better than his first wife. You're resolved then.'

Cavendish nodded. 'And there ain't no time like the present. I'll catch up with him at High Butte.'

'Watch your neck. The last *hombre* who tried out High Butte broke his,' Doc observed dourly.

Leaderless, Preacher's crew would not interfere in the matter of Irma's trial. There'd be no one to try and prevent Cavendish and Irma riding out just as soon as she'd been acquitted. Cavendish did not think Sloan would issue an open challenge whereas Preacher was crazy enough to do anything.

'Where in tarnation are you headed?' Bart demanded.

'You talk too much, old-timer.' Cavendish needed to be back before the scaffold was completed. Knowing this town they'd rush the trial through with unseemly haste. Digging in his heels, Cavendish rode out. Had he looked back he would have seen Sloan and Eden speculatively watching his departure.

'So where's he heading?' Sloan demanded.

'Damned if I know,' Eden rejoined. He scratched his chin. 'Maybe he won't be back,' Eden essayed.

'He'll be back,' Sloan replied with certainty. 'That woman has our sheriff hooked and that's for sure. He wasn't toting a gunny sack. He's planning to return for the trial.'

'Too bad. Things would have been easier with Cavendish out of town,' Eden observed.

Sloan nodded. 'You're right. But it's too much to hope that we've seen the last of that little squirt. No pint-size lawman is going to tell this town what to do,' Sloan continued venomously.

'That woman has got to hang.'

'Certainly. I'm as anxious as you to see justice done. The next thing we could have in Salt Creek is a crooked lawman working hand in glove with the local wideloopers.' Eden paused. 'I'm booking into the hotel until the trial is over.'

Sloan stared after Eden wondering whether it was possible that Eden was running scared. Did Eden suspect that Cavendish might try to drygulch him when he headed home?

Goddamnit, the answer had been staring Sloan in the face all along. Cavendish had left town in a hurry because he intended to drygulch Preacher. It made sense. Preacher was the most vocal opponent, and the opponent from whom Cavendish reckoned he'd have the most to fear.

Sloan's eyes narrowed. Salt Creek might not know it yet but the young cowhand gunned down by the rustlers had been none other than the youngest son of the railroad vice president. Word was that if the town didn't hang young Newman's killer Salt Creek would not see a railway track. With Irwin Kaye out of the picture there was a gap to be filled, and Sloan intended to fill that gap. He had heard the rumours concerning young Patrick Kaye, and did not believe for one minute that Kaye would make it safely back to the Triple Crown. Young Kaye, in Sloan's opinion, was lacking. Young Kaye had gotten his pa killed. Sloan grinned. One could say that Patrick Kaye had done him a favour.

'Damn bastard! One day that crazy little runt is going to run out of luck.'

The voice was laden with venom. Sloan recognized the voice as belonging to the telegraph clerk, Pole. There was still a faint scar above Pole's right eye, a reminder of the coffee pot hurled by an irate Sheriff Thomas Cavendish.

Seeing Pole gave Sloan an idea. Pole was a fool and that was for sure. At times Pole was a drunken bum.

'I could not agree more,' Sloan

agreed gravely. 'I'm sure the whole town shares your sentiment.' He bestowed a warm smile upon a bemused Pole. 'Let me buy you a drink. It's the least I can do, considering I was foolish enough to approve Cavendish's appointment.'

'That was a damn fool thing to do if you ask me,' Pole declared truculently.

'You are so right. Now, how about that drink? I feel I owe you. You could have lost an eye after all.'

Pole's face darkened. 'He had no right to do that. No right at all.'

'Right does not apply when it comes to Sheriff Cavendish,' Sloan murmured.

'A decent lawman would run that killer out of town,' Pole snorted. 'Instead of which Jack McGinley is . . . '

'We can forget about McGinley for the time being,' Sloan soothed, not wishing to see Pole side-tracked.

★ ★ ★

Cavendish had made good time, and he was pretty sure that he was ahead of Preacher. He thinned his lips. Preacher was asking to be taken down a peg or two and Cavendish aimed to oblige.

Cavendish studied the sloping shale-covered descent which led down to lower ground and the trail which would bring Preacher into his sights. Trouble was he had no head for heights. Just looking down made his stomach churn. But it had to be done.

'I ain't a quitter,' he muttered through clenched teeth, aware that he could not delay for he had spotted a moving speck far below and that speck must be the homeward-bound Preacher.

Cursing, Cavendish began his descent. Expressing his opinion of Preacher, he found, helped fuel his resolve. Shale disturbed by the horse began to slide downwards, slowly at first but gathering momentum as it moved. Dust filled Cavendish's nostrils and eyes causing him to realize he had been foolhardy in not using a bandanna to shield mouth and nostrils.

'Hell's bells, I thought you were not going to make it down in one piece,' Preacher observed gleefully. He conveyed the impression that he would have liked nothing better than to see Cavendish break his neck or even a limb. 'Last man who came down the Butte broke his neck,' he continued. 'He was drunk. You ain't drunk are you, Sheriff? Drunk with despair because I ain't aiming to relent? That woman is as guilty as sin. I'll see her hang.'

'Maybe I'm not here to ask you to reconsider,' Cavendish could not help but respond. 'Maybe I have an entirely different motive. Ever thought what that motive might be?'

There was an abrupt silence.

Cavendish realized he'd made an error of judgement when Preacher reached for his .45.

With a curse Cavendish launched himself at Preacher, snatching at his gun arm just as Preacher's hand was about to close over the butt of his .45.

Both men fell to earth with a jarring thud. But the fall was not sufficient to knock the stuffing out of Preacher, the old-timer fought desperately.

'I ain't here to kill you,' Cavendish hollered, knowing he had brought this upon himself. And in Preacher's case old bones did not break easily. Preacher had survived the fall unscathed. Yep, the Devil looked after his own when it came to Preacher.

'Then what the hell do you want?' Preacher attempted to knee Cavendish in the groin. 'I ain't afraid to meet my Maker,' he yelled.

Cavendish managed to hold Preacher down. With difficulty.

'John Gentle, I'm arresting you and holding you whilst I pursue my investigations!'

Preacher stilled. He stared up at Cavendish as though the lawman had taken leave of his senses. 'What the hell are you talking about, Cavendish?

What investigations?'

'I have reason to suspect your second wife didn't just disappear. I suspect you did away with her and I aim to investigate the matter.' Cavendish smiled unpleasantly and waited for the flood of denials and curses which were bound to follow his ludicrous announcement!

'How ..?' Preacher muttered. 'How did you . . . ?'

Aghast, Cavendish clapped a hand over Preacher's mouth. He did not want to hear. He knew what he had been about to say. Preacher was guilty. And maybe even prepared to confess. These were words Cavendish had no wish to hear.

Ruthlessly, Cavendish managed to stuff a bandanna between Preacher's yellow fangs. A second bandanna secured his mouth.

'I'm stowing you away until after Irma's trial.' Cavendish hauled Preacher to his feet. 'It'll give you time to reflect upon what you want to say. As you clearly ain't right in the head, I cannot take any confession you may care to make as genuine.' He shook his head. 'Come to think of it, Preacher, it would have been easier to blast you for resisting arrest. You're damn lucky I'm an honest lawman. And you're luckier still I ain't hearing too well today.'

★　★　★

Bart Parker had watched Cavendish ride out. It had occurred to Bart that maybe the lawman was after Preacher. Being a Cavendish the sheriff might have it in his mind to do away with him. Which was too bad, for the town would not be the same without him. For over twenty-five years, Preacher had been ranting and raving. It was hard to believe that he had ever been a man who kept his views to himself.

'What in tarnation are you up to?' Bart Parker demanded irritably.

Jim and his woman employee were

engaged in setting up a trestle table outside Bart's livery barn. With dexterity the woman proceeded to lay out pies.

Bart scratched his head. 'Am I dreaming? What's going on?'

'Seems like they intend having the trial this very day,' Jim replied.

'What the hell are you saying?' Bart demanded. 'The scaffold ain't even erected.'

'They aim to use one of your beams,' Jim volunteered.

'The hell they are. I ain't countenancing a hanging in my barn!' Bart yelled, enraged. 'Nor a pie table before my establishment.' Kicking out, he sent the table flying. Pies landing in the dirt.

'The whole town knows she's guilty.' Jim did not dare right the table.

'Ever seen a lynch mob?' Bart hollered. 'I have. It ain't a sight I ever want to see again.'

'They're sending for Gough,' Jim volunteered.

'The judge won't want to be tarred

with something like this,' Bart snorted. 'Gough's got ambition. This kind of fracas would ruin him.'

'Where's the sheriff?' The woman sniffed disapprovingly. 'That's what I want to know.'

'Damnation. Never thought I'd use Old Thunder on two-legged critters.' With surprising alacrity Bart disappeared inside his barn. He reappeared with an ancient buffalo gun under his arm.

'You can't stop them,' Jim argued. 'They're as drunk as skunks, most of them. Sloan's been buying. Sure as hell Cavendish didn't ought to have thrown that coffee pot at Pole. That man knows how to harbour a grudge.'

'Pole? What's a telegraph clerk doing mixing himself up in this?' Bart snorted.

'Pole and Mooney, they're the two fanning the flames.'

Bart spat. 'Pie tables indeed. Get out of my sight, Jim. I'm ashamed of you. Just you get before I turn Old Thunder on you.'

McGinley hastened towards Ivy Tucker's house cursing Tom Cavendish for not being around. He knew Clem's daughter: she'd go out to meet them rifle in hand. And maybe get herself shot.

The hotel clerk had been quick to fill McGinley in on what was going on in Salt Creek. The man had been taken aback by the way McGinley's face had whitened with fury when the clerk started on about the lynch mob over at the saloon, men who were getting liquored up to march to Miz Tucker's home.

'We'll see about that,' McGinley had snarled and rushed out.

Moss was also determined to do his damnedest to help Ivy Tucker. He tried to reason with the obstinate woman.

'Hand the girl over,' he advised. 'She's guilty after all. If your damn brother was not smitten he'd be the first to agree.'

'I'm ashamed of you, Joseph Moss.'

Ivy proceeded to check her rifle. 'If my pa was here now he'd kick you out. Us Cavendishes stand our ground. No matter what,' she concluded ominously.

'Where is she?' Moss demanded.

'Why, shut in the cellar. I don't want her getting shot. I promised Thomas I'd keep her safe and that's just what I aim to do.'

'You ain't going out there,' Moss yelled in desperation. 'Goddamn it, woman, I'll do it. I'll defend you.'

'I'll defend the house.' She tightened her grip on the rifle. 'You'll need to kill the leader. Take him out first. Men in this town are lacking.'

'Lacking!'

'They ain't got what it takes to stand firm and put their lives on the line,' she stated firmly. 'They care, you see. Especially the men with families. Pa always maintained most folk are sheep. And he was right. Don't look so glum, Joseph. Sheep scatter real easy.'

8

Unnoticed, Sloan fell back until he was at the tail end of the mob. The mood had yet to turn ugly. These men might be heading for a church picnic. With Cavendish out of town no one expected trouble. There was his sister, of course, but she was only a woman.

A considerable number of respectable, bonnetted womenfolk followed on behind the men. He smiled contemptuously. They would have something to natter about for many years to come. It was not every day a woman was hanged.

'Gough won't preside. He wants nothing to do with this,' the man Sloan had despatched for the judge reported back.

'Keep it to yourself,' Sloan ordered abruptly. Gough was not a necessity, although Gough's presence would have given the hanging an air of respectability.

Instead they must make do with a citizen's verdict. And what other verdict could there be. Rustlers were always hung; exceptions were not made. Sloan was not surprised by Gough's lack of enthusiasm. Wisely, the judge did not want to be associated with a livery-barn hanging.

Tomorrow these men would not want to look one another in the eye. Pole, Mooney and a good many others would have one hell of a hangover.

And they'd have Cavendish to face, and he was liable to go haywire. When that happened, Cavendish would put himself outside the law.

Sloan's thoughts digressed. He saw himself as a younger man driving his herd through Kansas. He'd staked his fortune upon the drive. He remembered how he had crossed into Missouri only to find legislation had been passed prohibiting the transportation of Texas beef.

The local herds had to be protected, they had said, and Texas cattle brought fever.

Sloan smiled bitterly. He had lost everything. But that was water under the bridge: he would not lose again. This town was going to be *his* town. He was going to pile up wealth beyond his wildest dreams.

If that goddamn railroad came to Salt Creek.

Pole swayed on his feet.

'We'll show the bastard,' he muttered, looking round for Sloan who had but a short time before been at his elbow. Now Sloan was nowhere to be seen. In Pole's muddled mind this was not about trying a rustler, this was about showing Sheriff Cavendish that he could not get away with treating honest, hard-working men as dirt. Why, Sheriff Cavendish had never done a day's work in his life. And as for what he was doing now, according to Mrs Pole, the sheriff was a disgrace. Pole, who wouldn't have minded a go at the girl himself, had agreed.

'Come on, come on,' someone behind shouted, and Pole staggered on towards Ivy Tucker's white-painted house.

Moss and McGinley had first met outside Ivy Tucker's house. The two now stood shoulder to shoulder before her white gate. Neither acknowledged the other. Both knew they had to save Cavendish's fool sister, because if they did not, Ivy Tucker could end up as dead as Cavendish's fancy.

Ivy Tucker had made the introductions until both men, losing patience simultaneously, had hollered at her to get the hell inside.

The sound of the marching, hooting, lynching party was drawing nearer. McGinley began to whistle. It was his habit to whistle when gunplay was imminent. Moss lit his pipe and clamped his teeth on the stem. Each hoped the other would take a bullet.

McGinley did not intend to allow Cavendish to forget how it had been he, Jack McGinley, who had stepped in and saved Cavendish's woman whilst Cavendish had been engaged upon some fool errand or other.

Although how it was that a fine, tall, attractive woman such as Irma could want Tom Cavendish was hard to fathom. McGinley chose to believe Irma must be playing Cavendish along.

'Don't shoot,' Moss advised, as a man rounded the corner. 'That's old Bart Parker from the livery barn. He hangs out with Tom so I reckon he's here to help.'

'I sure am,' Bart whispered. 'I've brought Old Thunder. That ought to scatter them.'

'Where is he, Bart? Where's Cavendish?' Moss enquired.

'Damned if I know,' Bart advised. 'Although he left town in a hurry.' Bart would not voice his suspicions concerning Preacher.

'Damned if I care,' McGinley drawled. 'He ain't needed.'

'Pole ain't a strong man,' Bart observed. 'And he's drunk! Mob's as strong as the man leading it. Pole is the wrong choice. Sloan should have chosen a better man. And as for Mooney it's a wonder he don't pass out.'

'So you suggest we kill Pole and they'll scatter!' McGinley smiled. 'Well, I reckon I can oblige.'

'There's no need to kill anyone,' Moss clenched his jaw. 'Unless it's forced upon us.'

'Of course, there's a need to kill someone,' Bart snapped. 'This is a lynch mob we're talking about. I've seen more than one lynching in my time and it's not a sight I'd recommend. Particularly, if they're lynching a young female. You can't miss Pole. Tall. Long ginger hair, thinning on top, long neck, popping eyes.'

McGinley nodded.

'He's a married man; he's got a wife and four children,' Moss volunteered.

'Then what's he doing leading a lynch mob?' McGinley actually grinned.

Pole felt proud. He was proud to lead the men through town. For the first time in his humble life he felt important. He was somebody, rather than a nobody.

His befuddled brain registered the presence of the three men before Ivy Tucker's house, but the men behind him kept moving and the momentum carried him forward. When he finally had to halt, the man at his back cannoned into him and sent him flying.

Moss grabbed the opportunity to avoid bloodshed.

'You damn fool, Pole,' he yelled, wanting all to hear. 'This ain't legal. You ain't fit to be let loose. You go on home now and sober up.' Purposely he headed for Pole.

'Damn fool,' McGinley observed, and he was not referring to Pole.

No one moved. No one made a move to stop Moss as he reached down, took up a handful of shirt and hauled Pole to his feet.

Moss was determined not to lose the initiative. He was confident the men could be turned from their purpose. Sloan, he saw, was not amongst the leaders. Having stirred the men up Sloan was keeping out of it.

'Shame on you,' Moss yelled. Swinging with his left hand he connected with Pole's chin.

Pole wasn't a fighting man; he was a telegraph clerk and that was all. Moss jabbed Pole in the stomach and then released him. Eyes glazing, Pole fell to the ground. Vomit spewed from his lips.

'You men go on home,' Moss ordered, as though there was no doubt that they would go home. 'We'll have the trial just as soon as the sheriff gets back. We'll do this right, we'll — '

A stone struck Moss upon the temple. With a grunt, Moss fell.

'Come on, men. I'm not the champion stone thrower of all Ireland for nothing,' Mooney whooped. 'Let's stomp the bastard. Ain't no one going to stop us . . . '

Mooney, although drunk, was not incapable nor was he as drunk as he should have been.

Men surged forward stepping over

the prone form of Moss, heedless of whether they stepped on him or not.

McGinley put an end to the nonsense. Moss was liable to be trampled until he was unrecognizable, Miz Tucker and her girls would be terrorized and the female wide-looper hanged so he merely did what he considered had to be done.

Raising his .45 McGinley calmly put a slug between the big Irishman's eyes. Regrettably, his reputation on this occasion was not sufficient to deter drink-sodden varmints.

'Was the champion stone thrower of all Ireland,' McGinley corrected calmly, breaking the silence which had suddenly descended. He did not give them time to rally or even think. 'Sure you can rush me if you have the stomach for it. But men will die. Who wants to be the next one? Step forward and I'll oblige.'

Bart Parker sighted Old Thunder. 'You men ain't upholding the law, you're breaking it. You're nothing better than a damn lynch mob. I should know, I've seen a mob in action. Yes, sir, and they hanged the wrong man. One of my kin.'

'He's shot Mooney,' a man observed in disbelief.

'Of course he has. This ain't a church picnic,' Bart snorted. 'And he had to do it, to save an innocent man. Joe Moss never harmed any man in this town.' Bart discounted Pole who'd been damn lucky: Pole was still alive. 'All he's guilty of is looking out for his intended which is right and proper. Shame on you men, scaring a poor widow-woman near to death. Now get on home now before anyone else dies needlessly.'

'Bart's making sense.' Out of breath, Doc had arrived. 'Besides which you can't hold a trial without a judge. Gough has rightly declined to preside over this shambles.'

'His *intended*? Goddamnit I've shot the wrong man,' McGinley jested. He eyed the assembled men with a gunfighter's eye. 'Make your minds up.

If anyone wants to die today I'll be happy to oblige you. This .45 ain't called a Peacemaker for nothing. It brings lasting peace.'

'I'm quitting! She can hang tomorrow.' A grizzled man left the crowd.

A second followed his example, and then a third.

'Hell, I'm not crossing McGinley!' Moss groaned.

'Too bad,' McGinley observed. 'He's still breathing.'

*　*　*

Patrick Kaye lost his horse. It went down beneath him taking him quite by surprise although a more experienced traveller would have known the animal had been pushed far too hard.

Kaye had been traversing rock flats; already exhausted and saddle sore he had not been paying close attention to his surroundings. His thoughts had been wandering, dwelling with pleasure upon the torture Cavendish would have to endure before he took his last breath.

And also, at the back of his mind, was the worrying thought that he ought never have started upon this foolhardy quest. He had a hell of a way to travel, a hell of a way to go and now he was not even sure he would even be able to find Mark Brain.

Cursing, Patrick struggled to his feet. His knee hurt like hell but at least he could stand. Nothing was broken.

'Goddamn you,' he screeched at his horse. 'Goddamn you to hell, you let me down!' He laughed harshly. He'd leave it to suffer he decided. There'd be no merciful end for this dumb critter.

There was high rock ahead to his left. And it occurred to him that he must get to the summit and scout out the lie of the land. He could maybe even light a signal fire in the hope that there was someone other than himself in this godforsaken wilderness.

Gritting his teeth, he struggled over the uneven jagged rocks enraged to discover there was a good deal of spiked shrub between himself and his destination. And, despite his endeavours to avoid them the damned spiked bushes managed to rip his duds and break his skin.

But the thought that death awaited any luckless *hombre* stranded out in this no-man's land was enough to keep him moving. Sweat trickled down his face and soaked his body beneath his already damp and stinking shirt. And his knee throbbed away unmercifully, the pain bringing tears to his eyes. But still he kept moving forward.

Reaching the summit, he collapsed with exhaustion to lie with his arms outstretched and his face pressed against burning red earth whilst the heat of the sun threatened to fry his brains, for his hat was down below with the horse.

As were his canteens.

Patrick Kaye let out a demonic howl for there was nothing out there, nothing to be seen, no sign of movement, no sign of any crude dwelling. He was quite alone.

And he did not know what to do. His pa had always been there telling him what to do. Now Pa was gone and he was in charge of himself.

Giving way to utter despair, he alternatively howled with pain or cursed Thomas Cavendish and his horse, even his own Pa for failing him.

All were wanting save himself.

*   *   *

'Time ain't improved your disposition I see!' McGinley observed, in a voice which decidedly lacked warmth. 'You ought to be down on your knees thanking me,' he added. 'I saved your woman's neck.'

'And blasted Mooney!' Cavendish exclaimed, ill pleased but forced to concede that Mooney, being a drunken bum, had brought misfortune upon himself.

McGinley shrugged. He gave a cool

171

smile. 'I had no choice. Maybe the thought of a mob stomping over me and the old-timer doesn't trouble you none but I value my hide.'

'So how's Moss?' Cavendish was loath to concede he owed McGinley, but undoubtedly he had saved Irma's life.

'Bruised and ashamed of himself.' McGinley grinned. 'As he should be. He ought to have known Mooney was the most dangerous of the pair.' McGinley paused. 'Whatever you were doing, Cavendish, you made an error. You ought never to have left that woman. You let her down!'

Cavendish studied his boots. McGinley spoke the truth.

'If it had been left to me I would have killed Pole before dealing with Mooney,' McGinley continued. 'And now that miserable varmint has repaid being shown mercy by wiring the fort. He's requested assistance.'

'How do you know?'

'Simple. It appears Pole's eldest boy

172

is sweet on Cissie. He spilled the beans. It seems his pa is still after your hide on account of that pot of coffee.'

'Damnation!' Cavendish swore softly.

'You ought to kill him,' McGinley advised.

'I'm a lawman.'

'No you ain't,' McGinley corrected. 'Right now you're a man taken with a woman, a woman who is guilty of cattle rustling and maybe killing, a woman who, by rights, ought to hang, and you're conspiring to see justice ain't done. I suggest you take the girl and get the hell out of Salt Creek pronto, immediately after this farce of a trial. I can guarantee that Gough ain't going to sentence her to hang. I can't guarantee that when the army arrives in Salt Creek they won't rule a mistrial. This town is gonna turn against you first chance it gets.'

Cavendish nodded. It was true: he could not deny it.

'Pole's accusing you of turning renegade, of throwing in your lot with wideloopers,' McGinley continued with enjoyment.

Cavendish thinned his lips. 'I ain't done nothing to deserve this.'

McGinley laughed. 'You damn fool, deserving ain't got nothing to do with this. This has got to do with the railroad. Or so I reckon. I hear tell Thaddeus Newman's boy died in Salt Creek. And Newman owns that damn railroad. Now do you see!'

Cavendish swore. He saw all too clearly.

★   ★   ★

'You damn fool!' Sloan raged, nostrils pinched with anger.

'I thought you'd be pleased,' Pole bleated.

'Yeah, me and Thaddeus Newman,' Sloan snarled, unable to stop himself.

'Thad — ' Pole began.

'In Salt Creek we take care of our own concerns,' Sloan gritted knowing it was too late to stop the army poking around into matters which did not concern them. 'Cavendish has broken no law. Damn it, he *is* the law.'

'But not for long,' Pole rejoined obstinately.

'You're a jackass, Pole. Get out of my sight.' Sloan controlled himself with difficulty.

'I could have been killed,' Pole whined. 'And Mooney was killed, shot down like a mad dog!'

'Well, it takes a mad dog to recognize another,' Sloan observed without sympathy. 'No doubt McGinley recognized that you were nothing but a damn, meddlesome telegraph clerk. Now get the hell out of my sight.'

'There ain't no call to take that tone of voice, Sloan. You put me up to heading the lynch mob and that's what it was, no doubt about it. And for what! Gough's getting ready to hear the case this very afternoon.' Pole smirked. 'I'm going, Rancher Sloan, but you ain't heard the last of this.'

Sloan stared after the departing

telegraph clerk the thought occurring to him that perhaps Pole ought to meet with an accident of the most serious kind. His departing words could have been interpreted as a threat. Maybe Cavendish would do him a favour and blast Pole, although with Cavendish one could not tell what the little varmint was liable to do.

Sloan's men were in town. Purposefully they were setting about making themselves conspicuous. Sloan hoped that a show of force would be sufficient to convince the doubters of Salt Creek that the right verdict needed to be rendered.

Sloan had also put the word out that Cavendish had killed Preacher. If Preacher was coming, he'd be here by now. Eden, to Sloan's disgust, had taken his men and left town. He held Sloan responsible for the lynch mob and couldn't understand why Sloan hadn't waited. Eden couldn't see Cavendish taking on the whole town to save the girl.

* ★ ★

Patrick Kaye had to drink. He was going mad. His tongue had swollen. Worse, his knee had swollen and his leg would not take his weight. He could not get back down to the horse and canteens of precious water.

High above, dark specks in a clear blue sky, buzzards circled.

'I ain't done for yet,' he hollered, as he shook his fist in a futile attempt at defiance.

Painfully he crawled back towards the edge; without hope he gazed down upon the harsh landscape below. And saw movement. His heart jumped. He was not mistaken; there it was: a small speck out yonder heading his way for, of course the speck was a horse and rider and the buzzards had signalled his presence more effectively than ever he could have done himself.

As if to reassure himself he touched the butt of his six-shooter. One horse wasn't going to tote the two of them out of here. Water and victuals for one were not going to sustain two.

Minutes passed. To young Kaye they seemed interminable, more like hours than anything else. And the spot grew bigger and bigger, finally materializing into an old-timer astride a burro.

The old-timer dismounted beside Patrick Kaye's downed horse. Sunlight glinted as the oldster pulled his gun. A shot reverberated and the animal was finally out of its misery.

Reaching into his back pocket, Patrick drew out a small hand mirror. He tilted the glass, caught the sun and directed the beam at the oldster. Raising a hand the old man shaded his eyes, squinted upwards and then waved.

'Halleluja, Halleluja,' Patrick yelled. He'd kill the oldster, take the burro and get himself home, back to the ranch and safety. No one could reasonably expect him to ride into the Badlands given the state of his throbbing knee. No one would think the worst of him for heading home but, they sure as hell would snigger when they saw him return on the damn burro. Why the hell couldn't the old coot have been riding a horse?

The old bastard was taking his time, pouring water into a shallow bowl and offering it to the burro. The sight enraged Patrick for his tongue was swollen and seemingly stuck to the roof of his mouth.

But then, finally, the old man started to clamber upwards. Patrick tried to stand up and then collapsed. Realization dawned. He was not in any fit state to plug the oldster and help himself to the burro. He needed his help to make it out of here alive.

But that didn't change matters at all. Saving his own skin had to take precedent over all else. He could almost here his pa, almost hear Irwin's voice giving approval.

'There's nothing else you can do!' Irwin would have said.

9

'I'm not giving you a choice, Gough.' Deliberately McGinley omitted to call him Judge. 'That female walks free or I spill the whole can of worms. Mrs Gough and all Salt Creek are going to know what you got up to. You hired my gun to kill your own — '

'That's enough. Lower your voice.' Gough was frantic. They were in the smoking-room of the hotel which would serve as a makeshift court. They were quite alone save for a lone fly which droned overhead.

'Dress it up in fancy words,' McGinley encouraged. 'You're the judge and allowed to use your discretion,' he paused. 'Just as I aim to exercise my own discretion concerning certain matters!' He paused. 'The sheriff is gambling the jury will acquit her, but if not, sentence that girl to hang and you'll face the consequences.' He grinned. 'I never bluff. I'll see you tarnished for the rest of your days. Even if it was all an out-and-out lie, mud would stick. Folk would whisper wherever you went, and Mrs Gough . . . '

'Leave my wife out of this,' Gough ordered angrily.

'And Mrs Gough, knowing you better than anyone else, will know I'm speaking the gospel truth,' McGinley sneered.

'I've already decided to show mercy,' Gough lied, unwilling to lose face.

'That ain't what you told the deputation which met you when you hit town.'

'Perhaps not. But I've reconsidered.'

'That's wise of you.' The fly landed on the table. McGinley brought his clenched fist down. 'Mind you are inclined to be merciful, or I'll swat you like this pesky fly.' Gough, he saw, was looking decidedly unwell. 'I'll bid you good day,' McGinley concluded cheerfully.

'May you rot in hell!' Gough hissed.

McGinley shrugged. 'I'll be in good company, Judge. There ain't no doubt about it!' So saying, he swaggered out, confident good old Judge Gough wouldn't be a problem.

Gough's chest hurt. The trial could go either way and if they found that girl guilty his sentence would cause uproar. He closed his eyes and imagined McGinley forcing his way to the front of the court, McGinley yelling out what had happened twenty years back.

Gough had actually asked for his money back. No way, McGinley had jeered, I was more than ready to carry out my side of the bargain and don't you forget it.

And it hadn't been worth it!

Maybe Sheriff Thomas Cavendish would find that out one day.

* * *

'There's a railroad man in town.' McGinley recognized the voice. It belonged to Pole.

He stood outside the hotel chinwagging. He had yet to see McGinley.

'He's here to see how Salt Creek upholds the law.'

McGinley stepped out of the hotel. Pole's back was towards him. Reaching out, McGinley shoved, and sent Pole sprawling in the dirt.

'Get out of my sight you varmint,' he ordered. 'I've no time for scum who try to lynch attractive women. I can think of a better use for them.' McGinley paused. 'And if I were Cavendish I'd fill you full of holes. Sure as hell you're pushing your luck, telegraph clerk!'

Pole, without rejoinder, scrambled to his feet and scuttled away.

Too bad, McGinley thought. Like all small towns, word spread, and word was Thaddeus Newman's boy had been killed by the wideloopers and if the girl did not hang, Salt Creek could say goodbye to the railroad. Cavendish might have pulled it off if it hadn't been for the lure of railroad wealth.

And the girl's confidence in Cavendish was vanishing, because she was now saying it would be better to go down in a hail of bullets than face a noose.

McGinley knew that he'd have to attend the trial and keep his eye on Gough the whole time. And from that stare Gough would know that if he put a foot wrong the truth would out. That damn fool Cavendish had waited too long. He was in a corner and knew it. Well, it was lucky indeed for Thomas Cavendish that he was here to take care of matters, McGinley reflected, and he was not going to let Cavendish forget it.

★   ★   ★

The old man squatted down by Patrick Kaye. And then the oldster opened his mouth to reveal he still possessed teeth. Mouth gaping, he continued to regard Kaye for a considerable length of time.

'So you're alive then,' he observed quite unnecessarily, 'and in a mighty bad way I'd say. What's gotten into you, boy, leaving that critter to suffer and leaving your canteens and victuals? Where are you from, boy?'

'Salt Creek,' Patrick croaked.

'The sun ain't fried your senses then,' the oldster observed. 'And where was you headed?'

'Badlands,' Patrick croaked, and the need to brag made him add, 'After Brain.'

'Going after Brain eh,' the oldster continued. 'Well, son, I guess I was mistaken, the heat *has* fried your brains after all. Now don't you fret none, I mean to help you; I'll get you back down and tend your leg. You can rest up with me. I've got water and victuals. Don't you fret, Betsy will get you down.'

'Betsy?'

'My burro.' The oldster whistled. 'And don't you be asking to buy Betsy because I'd rather die than part with her. That burro is a damn sight more reliable than any female I've known and I've known a good many. In my younger days I sure as hell did my utmost to emulate Brigham Young. Now there's a man to admire.'

'You talk too much, old-timer,' Kaye thought. He fashioned his features into what he hoped was a grateful smile. 'Thank you kindly,' he croaked.

'I'm forgetting myself. Here.' The oldster passed the canteen to Patrick. 'Drink slow. Let the water trickle slow down your throat and just thank your lucky stars you didn't get anywhere near Mark Brain. He ain't an *hombre* you'd want to know.'

The oldster was yarning, Patrick decided. They all did that. The crazy old coot was implying that he was acquainted with Mark Brain.

Kaye allowed the tepid water to trickle down his throat. Nothing had ever felt better. Naturally nothing had changed; he'd bide his time, wait until his leg would take his weight, and then he'd make his move. He'd help himself to that mule and the old coot would find his yarning days concluded.

*　*　*

Cavendish sat in his kitchen with Ivy, McGinley and Irma. His sister's voice droned on. Cavendish scarcely heard her. Wild thoughts filled his head of how he could get Irma out of town. Maybe he could grab Sloan and use the bag of wind for a hostage. Or maybe this railroad man everyone was talking about would be his best bet.

'There's no doubt about it, folk want to see a railroad running through Salt Creek. It will put the town on the map. They're going to find her guilty!' Ivy was saying.

'I say we shoot our way out,' Irma, who was sitting beside Cavendish, voiced her opinion.

McGinley grinned. He'd been waiting for this moment. They all knew Cavendish had misjudged the situation. Even Cavendish himself must see that this wasn't a situation he could handle. 'I've taken care of it. Gough ain't going to sentence her to death.' McGinley's voice oozed satisfaction. 'Trust me. I know what I'm doing, Thomas.' He winked at Irma. 'If I'd been the Sheriff of Salt Creek you would never have found yourself in this distressing situation, ma'am. Ain't that so, Ivy?'

Ivy, to Cavendish's annoyance, did not dispute the statement.

'Gough won't cast the first stone, he's a sinner just like the rest of us. Whatever the outcome, he'll not sentence Irma to hang.' McGinley winked again. 'Judge Gough made the mistake of hiring my gun. It was way back and I'll say no more. He ain't forgotten and neither have I.'

'Moss would make a fine sheriff,' Ivy reflected. She glanced at her brother., 'You'll have to leave, Thomas. You see that, don't you? You two must leave Salt Creek at exactly the right moment. No looking back. No lingering. Just ride. Bart's gonna have the horses ready and waiting.'

'What . . . ' Cavendish began but got no further.

'It's as plain as the nose on my face that I've got to do the thinking for you, Thomas Cavendish.'

'I couldn't have foreseen that Thaddeus Newman would take an interest in Salt Creek.'

'I hope you can foresee that certain folk intend to cause you problems,' McGinley observed. 'I'm thinking of Sloan and Pole, in particular.'

'The telegraph clerk?'

'You've made an enemy in Pole,' Ivy Tucker observed. 'Lord knows how this day will end, for I am sure I don't.'

'Gough wanted to postpone the trial!' McGinley announced. 'I said no.'

'Why . . . ?'

'Use your head, Cavendish. We want this over with before the army hits town.' McGinley shrugged, 'You'll just have to play the cards as they fall.' McGinley thought of the two Gough women. Those particular cards were falling nicely. Mrs Gough had all but promised to call at his room door tonight. Gough, it seemed, took a sleeping draught from time to time and . . .

Fists hammered on the door. 'You inside! Mr Sloan has sent us to escort the prisoner to the court. Are you ready, Cavendish?'

'Hell, as ready as I'll ever be,' Cavendish muttered.

'Just remember I'm the one they're fixing to hang,' Irma snapped.

Cavendish wasn't fooled. Naturally she was shaking in her boots.

'Ain't no one going to hang you, Irma,' he reassured her.

McGinley smiled. 'Not while I'm in town. Lucky for you, Thomas, your sister sent for me when she did. I've arrived just in time to save . . . '

Cavendish jerked open the front door. He confronted the two startled waddies.

'Get the hell out of my way,' he snarled. 'I ain't in the mood to appreciate an escort.'

For a moment it looked as if the two would argue, but then they backed down. 'Sure, Sheriff,' one murmured placatingly. 'We're just following orders. We'll tell Sloan you'll be along.'

'Do that!' Cavendish stared after them.

'They're scared of you!' McGinley rubbed his chin.

McGinley, Cavendish noticed was actually grinning as though he were enjoying himself. Maybe he was. McGinley was a crazy son of a bitch.

Cavendish squared his shoulders. 'Let's get to the damn court. I want this over with.'

Accusing stares followed him as they headed down Main Street towards the hotel. The mood in Salt Creek was definitely ugly. Cavendish actually felt as though he were the prisoner and not the lawman. McGinley whistled cheer-fully; Cavendish glowered. Irma cussed softly beneath her breath.

As they passed the scaffold she gripped Cavendish's arm.

'Pole has volunteered to do the hanging. He reckons you'll get cold feet.' Bart Parker joined the three. 'I've got them horses ready and saddled,' he hissed. 'My best. I kept them by especially.'

Cavendish nodded. He heard the words being bandied around, words such as 'murder' and 'Preacher'. Folk were drawing their own conclusions. Only Doc knew the truth and he was sworn to secrecy.

'You're a disgrace to your badge,' a woman screeched.

Sloan, Cavendish saw, was waiting outside the hotel. His face wore a smirk which made Cavendish want to put a fist into his mouth.

'So you're here, Sheriff,' Sloan observed grinning. He lowered his voice so that only Cavendish could hear. 'Let me tell you that you've done away with Preacher for nothing. You fooled us all, Sheriff Cavendish. We thought you were an honest lawman. When this is over, if you're still around, I'll see you pay for murdering Preacher.'

'Preacher ain't dead.'

'So he's alive and well is he?' Sloan sneered.

'Alive, yes.' As to being well, from the way Preacher was speaking then that was a debatable point. Preacher, it seemed, had strangled his second wife and buried her in an old mine shaft. Conveniently the shaft had caved in so it could never be known for sure whether Preacher was speaking the truth. Cavendish suspected Preacher's friends in town would judge him crazy and leave it at that. Justice, as far as Preacher was concerned, would not be done.

And it was lucky for Preacher that Cavendish was quitting as the sheriff of Salt Creek.

'I'm no fool, Cavendish,' Sloan retorted angrily, 'and I'll see justice prevails. I swear it.' He raised his voice delibertately. Looking round, Cavendish saw the stranger, a thin bespectacled *hombre* who could only be Newman's representative.

Feeling sick, Cavendish escorted

Irma into the makeshift court. Gough, looking decidedly unwell, was already seated. Cavendish glared at the assembled townspeople. Lawyer McNaught was prosecuting and Moss, of all people, was presenting the defence, a defence thought up by Cavendish himself. Irma's defence was that she had been forced to be with the rustling gang. Moss would argue that Irma had been taken forcibly from her home by one of them, Cavendish thinned his lips. There was no one around to dispute Moss, no one to say that Irma's gentleman friend had been one of the rustlers and she hadn't exactly been forced to ride with them.

Slater, the railroad man, observed that weaponry had not been handed in at the door. The men were all armed, some more than was acceptable in Slater's opinion. He was excited to see the legendary gunfighter, McGinley, was actually here in court. Thaddeus Newman was a great admirer of McGinley.

The tall redheaded killer had chosen to lounge quite close to Judge Gough and was even now busily engaged in whittling at a piece of wood. Gough, whose temper was known to be explosive, was surprisingly quiet.

'We hang murdering scum in Salt Creek,' the rancher who had identified himself as Sloan, observed loudly, as he took his place beside Slater. 'Females included. Mr Newman need have no worries on that score.'

'Excellent,' Slater murmured. Privately he thought the tall prisoner, quite inappropriately dressed in man's garb was a fine-looking woman. And there beside the prisoner was the loathed Sheriff Cavendish, short, balding and insignificant — if it were not for the two pearl-handled Colts he had chosen to wear.

'There's Gough's wife and daughter. Now they're what I call fine ladies,' Sloan observed.

The fine ladies, Slater observed, were regarding McGinley with interest.

'Steps are being taken to have Sheriff Cavendish removed,' Sloan continued, 'quite soon.'

'I see.' Slater did not quite see. But he expected all would be made clear in the progress of time.

Gough brought down his hammer violently.

'It appears the main prosecution witness, John Gentle, is not in court.'

'Your Honour' — Sloan was on his feet — 'there are concerns for John's safety. I have reason to believe he could be dead.'

'And we all know who killed him.' Pole jumped to his feet and shook his clenched fist in the air.

'Order,' Gough yelled, and pandemonium broke out as folk hurled accusations, most of them directed towards the sheriff.

'That's enough of such foolishness.' Doc was on his feet and shouting, 'I know for a fact that Preacher is alive and well.'

'Then why isn't he in court, Doc?

The whole town knows wild horses wouldn't have been able to keep Preacher away today. The only thing which could have stopped him would have been a bullet. Answer that if you can,' Sloan challenged, confident there could be no satisfactory answer.

Doc cleared his throat. 'You'll all be saddened to hear Preacher is temporarily insane.'

'Are you trying to tell us he's mad?' Sloan demanded.

'We know it already,' someone guffawed, 'but that does not make him loco.'

'The court will accept John Gentle's illness as a reason for non-appearance,' Gough ruled. 'And now, if no one has any objections, we'd best get the jury sworn in. And please remember, gentlemen, I will not countenance troublemakers in my court.' He looked at Pole as he spoke.

Cissy Tucker blew her nose loudly.

Two of Sloan's men grabbed Pole.

'Throw him out. The judge is right,'

Sloan declared. 'As the whole town knows, that stringbean of a telegraph clerk is a natural-born troublemaker.'

'This, is a trial for rustling and murder, not a comedy show,' Gough rebuked.

'Quite right, Judge, quite right,' McGinley drawled. 'Now let's get on with it!'

Cavendish stared hard at the jury. None of them would meet his eye. The atmosphere within the packed room was taut. Also the place was beginning to stink of sweat, tobacco and whiskey.

His gaze lingered on the railroad man. Thaddeus Newman's hireling.

David Slater, catching the sheriff's hard, calculating gaze, felt decidedly uneasy.

'Damnation!' Cavendish muttered. Ivy Tucker was not in court, and Cissie could only be here because her ma had sent her.

'You'll know when the time is right.' Cavendish recalled his sister's words. Sweat beaded his brow. 'Pa had an answer for everything,' Ivy had said.

Well that was true enough and Clem Cavendish's answers had tended to be short, sharp and violent.

Desperately, Cavendish endeavoured to catch Jack McGinley's eye. He succeeded, but McGinley clearly misinterpreted the message.

Pull yourself together man, McGinley mouthed silently.

Cissie grinned at her uncle.

Lord, she knows, Cavendish realized. She knows what her ma is gonna do. He signalled his niece, but she chose to ignore him.

What was he going to do? If Ivy made a mistake she'd be done for. She was going to emulate Pa, whose tales had not been yarns: they'd been factual accounts of violent deeds.

'You're looking decidedly queasy, Cavendish,' Irma hissed.

Cavendish took a steady breath. He must put his faith in Ivy. Once her mind was set she would not be deterred from her purpose. Ivy's only weakness had been Hiram Tucker and Lord knew that was a weakness she had overcome.

Irma's eyes were glued on Cavendish. She cursed herself for being a fool. She'd believed him, but the sight of the scaffold ready and waiting had shaken her faith, that and the fact that Cavendish had handed her a loaded .45 to conceal beneath the heavy plaid shirt she was wearing. He had not needed to say that if it came to it they must rely on their Peacemakers to save the day.

'I'll see things right,' Ivy Tucker had reassured her. Irma eyed Cavendish. From his expression she had a hunch that the sheriff knew what his sister was about. Ivy Tucker, Irma reflected was an unusual woman. Irma had heard mention of Hiram Tucker, and then there had been that business at the saloon, the sudden death Sheriff Cavendish had chosen not to investigate, behaviour which had recommended Cavendish to her.

Why trouble yourself, she thought as

she listened to Moss launch the defence.

'It's a bundle of lies,' Moss griped. He was only defending her because Ivy Tucker had insisted he be of use in Thomas's hour of need.

And Judge Gough was paying scant heed to Moss's laboriously presented defence. Gough knew darn well she was a widelooper although she had not shot the young puncher, the man who had fired that shot having gone down in a hail of bullets.

Preacher hadn't taken prisoners; wounded men had been blasted. He'd spared her because she was a woman. At the time she hadn't realized Preacher's only reason for sparing her was because he wanted to see her hang. Fortunately, or unfortunately depending how one looked at it, she, according to Cavendish, bore a resemblance to Preacher's murdered second wife.

McGinley snapped the piece of wood he'd been working on. Hell, he reflected, this could be his last day on earth because he was pretty damn sure there was not going to be a satisfactory conclusion to this matter. Rancher Sloan had far too many men in the court. Sloan had a contingency plan, and all to impress the railroad man. Unconsciously, McGinley flexed his fingers. He was glad to see Ivy Tucker was not in court. He would not have to worry about her taking a stray bullet.

'Do you need to consider your verdict?' Gough asked the jury, knowing full well consideration would not be necessary. They were going to find her guilty. He could read the signs. He had presided over enough trials. And, damn it, she was a rustler. Reluctantly he turned his head and met the mocking gaze of McGinley. Only a bullet would shut McGinley up and Gough could not commit murder in his very own courtroom.

'No, your Honour. We're of one mind. She's as guilty as sin,' the foreman announced.

'As are we all, wouldn't you say,

Judge?' McGinley observed loudly.

'In normal circumstances,' Gough declared, 'I would have no hesitation in pronouncing the death penalty, but having regard to the unfortunate woman's sufferings at the hands of her captors I intend to release her into the custody of Sheriff Thomas Cavendish. I believe an ayslum is the right place for this woman and I charge the sheriff to convey her — '

'You can't do it. Damn you, this is a hanging offence.' Sloan was on his feet.

Cissie Tucker left the courtroom. Planting herself in the middle of Main Street, Cissie loudly blew her nose.

'And if anyone is not in their right mind, it's you, Judge Gough,' Sloan challenged. 'You assured me justice would be done.'

'And it will be done,' Gough croaked, wondering how this was all going to end. Things were getting ugly.

McGinley's eyes were fixed on Cavendish who stood as if rooted to the spot, waiting. Irma's eyes were on

Cavendish as if awaiting a signal and . . . and suddenly McGinley understood: Ivy Tucker had been rambling on how men were useless and she'd need to sort matters herself . . .

The explosion rocked the room. It sounded as though it was next door although that was impossible. The chandelier crashed down from the ceiling and the mirrors tumbled from the walls as women screamed.

A second explosion followed. Pandemonium broke out with men and women shoving and clawing to get out as they surged towards the narrow doorway.

'Don't move, stay put.' McGinley shoved Gough's wife and daughter back against the wall. 'The hotel ain't coming down around our ears,' he advised. 'Stay put,' he reiterated. 'You'll be trampled if you try to get out.'

Needless to say this was Cavendish and Irma's time to get out!

McGinley saw they had joined the exodus, Cavendish using the butt of his

Colt to force a way through. The tide swept them along, through the narrow doorway and out of McGinley's sight. He had a hunch that it would be a mighty long while before he saw Sheriff Thomas Cavendish again.

10

On Main Street, folk milled around. Debris had been hurled far and wide and the glass fronts of establishments blown out.

Cavendish knew what his sister had done. She'd dynamited the church and the schoolhouse, providently both buildings being empty. Grabbing hold of Irma, Cavendish headed in the direction of the livery barn. It was time to get away before folk came to their senses.

A lone figure emerged from the dust cloud which hovered over Main Street. Hair askew, the 'lunatic', gun in hand, barred their path.

'You ain't gonna get away with this, Sheriff Cavendish!' Pole yelled.

Without hesitation, Cavendish put a bullet into Pole's right leg. Screaming in agony, the telegraph clerk went down. Nor had Pole what it took to sight his .45 and fire after the fleeing couple.

'Lord!' Bart Parker hollered. 'It seems like the Fourth of July has come early. Get the hell out of Salt Creek before folk get around to remembering your existence.'

'I ain't arguing!' Cavendish and Irma raced towards the livery barn, Pole forgotten.

Sloan fought his way out to the street. 'Get after them!' he yelled. 'Goddamn you, Pole! You could have stopped them.' He kicked out viciously at the wounded man.

Pole raised his head. He was bleeding to death. Blackness swam before his eyes. Making a tremendous effort he raised his .45 and squeezed the trigger. More by luck than anything else his bullet struck Sloan in the small of the back.

With a groan, Pole lost consciousness.

'You all saw it,' Doc shouted. 'A tragic accident. The man's gun discharged as he passed out.'

'It's Gough,' someone hollered. 'He's having a heart attack.'

'Goddamn it, I must see to Pole first. Sloan's beyond help.' Doc met Slater's eye. Slater was giving nothing away.

'I had better contact Thaddeus,' Slater murmured.

'You do that,' Doc's tone was curt. Feverishly he worked on Pole's leg.

'How is he?' Slater enquired.

'He'll be crippled the rest of his days,' Doc sighed. 'Why couldn't he just stick to sending telegraphs?'

'He had my church destroyed. And his accomplice may still be in town. A wolf in sheep's clothing,' the pastor raved.

'Swear me in, and I'll investigate,' Moss needed a job. 'Cavendish won't be coming back. Not unless the army brings him. And I can't see there's a need. Sentence was passed. Cavendish is only carrying out the sentence.' Moss eyed the assembled townsfolk, 'You need a local man for this job. A man who will always look favourably on the old residents as opposed to the carpet-bagging newcomers the railroad's gonna bring.'

'That's jumping to conclusions,' Dyers stated thoughtfully wondering whether he and Moss could do business. With Cavendish it would have been out of the question. He had always been an honest lawman except for this particular incident. And he couldn't be blamed for falling for a pretty face.

'This town has seen enough trouble,' Moss stated persuasively.

'Well, none of it was Cavendish's doing,' Bart Parker exclaimed heatedly.

'Let's just say Cavendish wasn't up to the job of dealing with the likes of Irwin Kaye.'

'I say we appoint Moss, or we'll have the army running Salt Creek!' Jim declared. 'There's nothing they'd like better than make this town eat humble pie. We don't need them and we don't want them.'

'Thaddeus Newman won't want to

209

do business with an army town,' Slater observed.

'Why?' Bart demanded.

Slater ignored the old man. 'You defended that girl, why?' he addressed Moss.

'Because he was paid handsomely.' McGinley joined them on the sidewalk. 'Judge Gough needs you, Doc, Real bad.'

'I'm about finished here.'

'That's a damn lie,' Moss said, but no one was listening.

'Swear him in.' Slater made the decision. Moss was a man Thaddeus Newman could deal with.

'And your first task, Sheriff,' Slater said, once Moss had been sworn in, 'is to raise a posse and pursue Sheriff Cavendish. At the least, you need to question him about the events here in town, the dynamiting of the church and school.'

Moss fingered his badge. 'That ain't hardly necessary, Mr Slater. I'd say a widelooper must have gotten into town.

This is his way of paying the town back. I can vouch for Cavendish; he had no hand in this.'

'We don't want him back,' someone wisecracked. 'Salt Creek wants the peaceful old days back again, and with Cavendish in town that just can't be.'

'Mr Newman will want to speak to your old lawman and the girl,' Slater advised.

'Then he'd best go get them himself,' Slim Jim rejoined. 'Railroad or no railroad, men of Salt Creek ain't risking their necks by pursuing Cavendish.'

Slater nodded. 'Mr Newman is a businessman. He's obliged to follow the best route. He has shareholders to consider, deadlines to meet. Whether the railroad comes through will have nothing to do with the girl or Cavendish.'

'That ain't what I heard,' Lawyer McNaught snapped.

Slater shrugged. 'You heard what Thaddeus implied. And then you drew your own conclusion.' Slater paused.

'Very likely Mr Newman will look for Sheriff Cavendish himself. Mr Newman never lets matters drop. You might do well to remember that.'

Bart Parker voiced the thoughts of them all. 'Damn bastard,' he said.

★ ★ ★

The old man had developed a hearty dislike for Patrick Kaye. And he knew with certainty what kind of man Patrick was. A demon lurked beneath the pleasant mask Patrick had chosen to adopt. He was aware that Patrick was merely waiting until his swollen knee was mended. The oldster had been treating the knee with an assortment of poultices and he had kept Patrick fed and watered, although he was sure this was going to prove to be a waste of time.

The old-timer knew that Patrick intended to kill him and steal Betsy just as soon as he was well enough to travel. From time to time he tried to warn

Patrick Kaye not to take the irreversible step.

' 'Vengeance is mine, sayeth the Lord',' he cackled. 'But I don't hold by such rubbish. Those who try to do me wrong, well, I make them pay. Believe me, boy.'

The trouble was, of course, that Patrick didn't believe him, although from time to time the mention of vengeance would launch a tirade directed at one Thomas Cavendish, a no-account lawman and Patrick's bitter enemy.

The old man irritated Kaye. He yarned daily, telling tales that only a fool would believe, and Patrick Kaye was not a fool!

* * *

Thaddeus Newman studied the reports received from Salt Creek. A frown furrowed his brow. According to Lieutenant Phillips, who had been sent to investigate certain irregular occurrences at Salt Creek, the towns-people the lieutenant had spoken with had insisted Cavendish had been doing a mighty fine job and no one had any complaints.

A new man, Moss, had been appointed as sheriff. And Judge Reginald Gough had suffered a fatal heart attack whilst carrying out his duty.

Not being a fool, Thaddeus Newman recognized that Judge Gough had either been bribed or blackmailed into setting the female outlaw free, albeit in a roundabout kind of way.

'I intend to conduct my own enquiries,' Lieutenant Phillips reported. Needless to say his enquiries would lead nowhere.

Thomas Cavendish was something of an enigma to Thaddeus Newman, a man who did nothing whilst the jail was burnt down. And he would have known the church and school were going to be blown to smithereens. Thaddeus, however, was not interested in Cavendish's accomplice; it was the lawman who interested him. Men had been killed in

Salt Creek, and Cavendish's name kept cropping up.

Thaddeus Newman decided to organize a hunting party. Every year he hunted with a parcel of wealthy friends. Big game was on the menu. This year they would be after something different. Thaddeus decided they would hunt down the runaway sheriff of Salt Creek. Although not exactly wanted by the law, Cavendish had run off with a convicted felon and Newman would bet his last dollar she'd never see the inside of Beauville Ayslum.

'I intend to return the girl and the sheriff to Salt Creek. I expect there will be a retrial.' Thaddeus put the idea to a group of his most trusted friends. They had been friends from college and called themselves the 'Lone Wolves'. All were wealthy and successful, and most importantly of all, one was an army man of some importance.

The idea mooted by Thaddeus was that troopers who had been cooped up, bored and drunk, with nothing to do now nearly every redskin had been exterminated, would be put to use blockading the way north, with orders not to apprehend Cavendish but to direct him southwards, back towards Salt Creek.

'I have a mind,' Thaddeus said, as he raised a glass of wine to his lips, 'to add Cavendish and the woman to my private collection.' Newman had hunted aboriginals in Australia and had taken many skins. He had also hunted in Africa. He had two collections: one for private viewing, consisting of the standard subjects, lions, tigers, bears and elephants; the second private collection was, strictly private.

★　★　★

'So you're personally acquainted with Mark Brain, are you, old-timer?' Patrick approached the old man with a smile upon his face.

It was time, to leave!

'Sure am,' the oldster chuckled. 'He's

a discriminating fella. And likeable most of the time. Fact is, he's married to one of my young ones. Leastways I think she's one of mine. I've got so many I can't count . . . '

'Sure old-timer, sure,' Patrick agreed patronizingly.

'They have to be real bad 'uns before Mark Brain gets near them. Mrs Brain insists upon it. She insists he mends his ways and — '

'To hell with you and your yarns, you lying old bastard.' Patrick hauled out his .45. 'You ain't never been anywhere near Mark Brain. The only fool around here is you.'

'I ain't no fool,' the old man protested in his quavering voice.

'The hell you ain't!' With a sneer, Patrick Kaye squeezed the trigger.

'I reckon you'll beat me there.' The oldster hauled out his own weapon and pointed it at Patrick. 'Mine's loaded, boy. Your's ain't. From the first I reckoned you intended to abuse my hospitality.' He waved the gun. 'Now don't you make a move or I'll blast off both legs.'

'I just need the burro. I'll pay real well,' Patrick blustered, sensing the old-timer was not going to shoot him down as he had first anticipated.

'Lie down.' The gun moved slightly.

'Why?'

' 'Cause. I aim to hog-tie you, that's why. I ain't fool enough to give you a second chance to commit murder. Now you lie down like I say, or I'll blast your legs and leave you here to die.'

Patrick lay down. He had a chance then. Surely he could kick out or grab the oldster. Old bones broke easily and old hands were slow to tie knots.

But the old man did not approach him immediately. Instead he whistled and clucked his tongue. The burro, Betsy, came ambling over. She headed straight towards Patrick.

'What the hell!'

He felt the hoof lightly touching the back of his head.

The old man cackled and now to

Patrick the laugh seemed to possess an insane quality.

'I told you Betsy was more reliable than any female. Fact is, females end up feeling sorry for folk and just can't be trusted to pull the trigger. But not Betsy. If I were to give the signal she'd squash your skull just as if it were an egg. Why, she'd splatter your brains far and wide.' The oldster tied Patrick's ankles together. 'But the fact is you ain't got brains. I tried to warn you to leave me be but you just wouldn't listen. Now stretch those arms in front of you. And don't you twitch whilst I'm binding your wrists because if you do Betsy will know what to do. Trained her myself, and all it took was a handful of sugar.'

Patrick Kaye did not dare twitch. The crazy old buzzard wasn't joshing.

'That's an odd ring you're wearing, boy. Where'd you get it?'

'I found it,' Patrick lied. 'You can have it if you like it. Take it.'

'I wouldn't touch that ring with a

219

ten-foot pole. That's a dead man's ring you're wearing, boy.'

'What do you aim to do with me?' The hoof was abruptly removed and the burro ambled away.

'Why, I don't aim to do a damn thing to you, boy. It ain't my intention to harm a hair of your head.'

'Then what is your intention?' With difficulty Patrick came to his knees. 'You can't keep me this way for ever.'

'That's not my intention either. I aim to see you succeed in your quest. Two of Brain's men will be along by and by. I aim to suggest they escort you to meet their boss. I wasn't lying, boy. Fact is he's my son-in-law, not that I readily admit to the fact considering Mark's peculiarities. I've decided to help you on your way. But don't thank me, son, I ain't doing you a favour.'

'Are you gonna tell him what I tried to do?' Patrick's voice shook.

'Nope. Telling tales ain't for men.'

Then there's hope for me yet, you old goat, Patrick thought. First thing he'd do next time round was blast that damn burro. And then he'd force the oldster to eat burro stew and burro steaks and Lord knows what else. That would hurt the old coot a darn sight more than any bullet. And at the end Patrick would slit the old fella's gizzard and . . .

'From the look on your face, boy, I reckon you've more in common with Mark Brain than you imagine.'

'You can't begin to know what I'm thinking,' Kaye retorted with false bravado.

The oldster cackled again. 'And you can't begin to know what I'm thinking, boy.' And it was just as well.

*   *   *

Irma and Cavendish had given up sharing a bedroll, but it wasn't because Cavendish didn't have a mind to share. Clem Cavendish had always assumed folk were out to get him and generally he'd been right. Cavendish was now assuming likewise that something was very wrong. And as yet he had not been able to fathom out what was going on.

'We've got to keep our wits about us Irma. We can't afford to relax our vigilance.'

'That last army patrol could have killed us and you know it. We ran right into them and they shot short. So what do you think?' She did not give him a chance to answer. 'I think Thaddeus Newman is behind this, Tom. He's got the money and it looks like he's got the power!'

'Maybe,' Cavendish agreed. 'There ain't no one in Salt Creek interested in us that's for sure!' He was thinking of Preacher.

Cavendish continued to toss dried vegetables into the stew pot. 'Fact is, Irma, we're being herded like sheep, back towards Salt Creek and the Badlands. That ain't necessarily bad. I know the Badlands. Pa was kind of taken with the place. They saved his life on more than one occasion. Could be they'll save us if we're being hunted.

And I reckon we are. Hell, I wish I knew what was in Newman's mind if it is him behind this.'

'Maybe it's best we don't!'

'We'll head back towards Garland,' Cavendish decided. 'Maybe Duffy will know what's going on.'

'But you shot the telegraph clerk.'

'So I did. But Pole ain't the only one who can work the wires.'

* * *

Red Antelope, the tracker, sat with Sheriff Duffy. The two were acquainted.

'This is a bad business,' Duffy ruminated. 'I ought to kill you, but they'd only get themselves another tracker. Lord knows I can't blast every tracker in the territory.'

As Duffy was speaking, the door of his office opened and a dust-weary Cavendish, followed by the girl, walked in.

'Talk of the devil!' Duffy exclaimed excitedly, jumping to his feet. 'And here he is!'

Red Antelope did not move a muscle. He simply stared at the man he'd been hired to hunt down.

'Tom Cavendish,' Duffy declared, 'let me introduce you to Red Antelope. He's been hired to hunt you down. He's waiting for Newman and his fine friends. They're expected day after tomorrow.'

'Lord!' Irma reached for her gun, but Cavendish forestalled her by grabbing her gun arm. 'What the hell!'

'Easy!' Cavendish advised. 'He's been hired to hunt us down. He ain't been hired to kill us. Ain't that so, Red Antelope?'

Red Antelope nodded.

'If he were to kill us, which is unlikely, he'd not get, paid, ain't that right, Duffy?'

Sheriff Duffy nodded. 'Sure is. Newman's imported fancy telescopic rifles. He's got servants along to cook the victuals and do the waiting. It beggars belief.'

Cavendish regarded Red Antelope.

'And what about Miss Irma? Were you hired to hunt her down?'

'No mention was made of the woman.' Red Antelope paused. 'I do not hunt women.'

'Thank you,' Irma replied sarcastically.

'Because they ain't worthy of his skills,' Cavendish explained. 'You've been paid then.'

'Before we leave,' Red Antelope replied.

Cavendish shrugged. 'Hunt me down if you can, but stay out of the rest of it. I'm loath to kill one of Duffy's friends but . . .'

'Do you think you could kill me?'

'Well, I ain't of a mind to find out unless pressed,' Cavendish rejoined. 'If Newman asks, tell him from me if he goes into the Badlands he won't come out. Being forced to eliminate men I don't even know weighs on my conscience. But it's them or us.'

'Thaddeus Newman never gives up,' Duffy observed dolefully.

Cavendish shook his head. 'There's

more to this than wanting justice for his dead son. Newman is enjoying himself.' He paused. 'We're checking into the hotel. Miss Irma needs a long hot soak and so do I. And I aim to wire Salt Creek. Maybe Miz Tucker may have some relevant information.' He shook his head. 'There's no point in trying to keep it secret we're here. I bet you when Newman hits town a whole parcel of folk just bursting to tell him I've passed through. I'm known here. And I caught the looks as we rode in, Irma.'

'You're crazy, Tom,' Irma rejoined. 'What's to stop this Indian — '

'No. He's a tracker. He ain't no Jack McGinley hired to kill folk who've never done him wrong. I just hope my sister . . . ' Cavendish shook his head. 'Well, there's just no reasoning with Miz Tucker, or certain Indian trackers. Both are as obstinate as mules.'

★ · ★ · ★

Ivy Tucker sighed. She stood on the sidewalk and watched as Newman rode out. McGinley had paid for Cissie's education but then he had left town saying he felt duty bound to see Mrs and Miss Gough safely back home. He was not interested in preventing Newman from pursuing Thomas.

Moss chewed on a straw. Jack McGinley had spent his last night in Salt Creek at Miz Tucker's house. Moss did not dare comment.

'Ain't you worried,' he finally asked, 'about Thomas?'

'Worried sick,' she replied. And with good reason. Preacher had been talking. About a certain locked room in Thaddeus Newman's mansion. Newman's son had divulged a few family secrets.

'Preacher's rambling a good deal these days,' Moss observed. He knew what was worrying Ivy. 'I reckon Newman is a darn sight worse than Mark Brain,' Moss concluded. 'If it's true!'

'Thomas can deal with Newman,' Ivy stated with certainty. She'd wired Garland. By now Thomas would know of Thaddeus's private collection.

★ ★ ★

Thomas Cavendish eyed Red Antelope. It was time to leave. Cavendish grinned humourlessly. 'A word of warning, Scout, you'd make a fine addition to a certain private collection.' He knew it was useless to try and dissuade the Indian. And as Duffy said, Newman could call in another tracker. 'You may care to ask one of your party about Thad's collection, or you may not!' Cavendish shrugged. 'Let's just say there's certain well-connected folk a darn sight worse than Mark Brain. From what I hear Brain only goes after them who do him wrong.'

11

Duffy did not bother to get up when a man who could only be Thaddeus Newman burst into his office. Instead Duffy clamped a cigar between his teeth and waited.

Newman was certainly an impressive man. Inner strength and self-confidence enveloped the man making it clear that here was a man not to be messed with. Cold, contemptuous eyes surveyed him.

'So you're Duffy,' Newman said without preamble.

'You know I am,' Duffy rejoined. Anyone seeing and comparing the two men, Newman and Cavendish, would doubtless put their money on Newman for there was nothing impressive about Thomas Cavendish's appearance.

'Cavendish's friend!'

'Yep,' Duffy agreed.

'For a friend you seem remarkably

unconcerned,' Newman stated.

'I'm betting on Cavendish.' Duffy rejoined. 'And as far as I know he ain't a wanted man.'

'He's wanted by me.' Newman smiled coldly. 'I'm insisting upon a retrial. Gough was seriously ill at the time . . . '

'Ain't no way you're returning Cavendish and the girl to Salt Creek,' Duffy interrupted. 'The fact is, Newman, if you persist in this foolishness, if you go on after Thomas you won't be coming back.'

'Do you know something I don't?' Newman challenged.

Duffy shrugged. 'It's common knowledge the late Clem Cavendish was a deranged killer. Not that I've ever said so to Thomas . . . '

'What the hell are you blabbing about?' Newman interrupted angrily.

'Well, I reckon Clem learned Tom everything he knew.' Duffy rubbed his chin. 'Yes, sir, Mr Newman, Clem Cavendish was your kind of man. Clem liked to collect ears so I've heard!' Duffy met Newman's gaze without flinching. Newman was startled but hiding it well. 'But old Clem never killed without good reason. And it would be beneath him to go gunning for a female. You accuse him of running a vendetta against a female and Clem would take it as an insult.'

'You speak as though the man's still around.'

'Well, I reckon he is in spirit,' Duffy rejoined, 'guiding Tom to do right, right by Clem's way of thinking that is.'

Newman snorted. 'I'm here for my tracker. Word is you've locked him away. If you think to dissuade me, Duffy, think again. I want that Indian and I want him now.'

Duffy shrugged. 'Red Antelope ain't locked away. True, he's bedded down in one of the cells, but the door ain't locked. You don't know Red Antelope, Mr Newman, just as you don't know Tom Cavendish . . .'

Ignoring the lawman, Newman jerked

open the door which separated the office from the cells. Newman disappeared through the door and Duffy heard him soundly berating Red Antelope.

Duffy grinned slightly. That was a mistake if Newman did but know it. Red Antelope did not take kindly to insults.

'Tell me, Scout,' Newman commanded, 'why the hell didn't Cavendish fill your red hide full of lead? What kind of yellow-belly is he?'

'Cavendish knows I will follow him. He does not fear you, Mr Newman.'

Newman's smile was wolfish. 'Then he should. Now get your butt down to the livery barn. Show me that you can earn your money.'

Red Antelope nodded. 'So be it.' The scout knew he'd be expected to cover four times the ground as his travelling companions. They'd ignored him and should a mishap occur which rendered Red Antelope a liability they would leave him to die. Red Antelope held them in contempt.

Should his employers become a danger to him he would leave them to fend for themselves. He was not dumb enough to give his last mouthful of water to save any one of them.

When they reached the livery barn the other members of Thaddeus's hunting party cursed him soundly. Red Antelope bore the insults in silence. He had expected them.

★　★　★

From time to time, Irma glanced at Cavendish. They were travelling at a steady pace, heading due east, and Cavendish did not seem as disturbed as he should have been considering their perilous circumstances.

'You're not betting on Newman, are you?' he enquired, catching her troubled gaze.

'It shows, huh?' Irma responded. 'Let's face it, Cavendish, Thaddeus Newman gets what he wants. He wants me dead and you too, Thomas. He won't give up. That's what Duffy said, Newman never gives up. That's why he's where he is today.'

'Thaddeus Newman is heading for certain death,' Cavendish replied grimly. 'I know he won't quit. In fact, his determination to run us down will be his ruin.'

Irma shrugged. 'I can't see you dealing with Newman, Thomas. You're one man. Lord knows how many he's toting along with him.'

Cavendish shrugged. 'Well, their deaths won't weigh on my conscience. Those men deserve to die. They're as bad as Newman. Must be, or they wouldn't be hunting with him. It's us or them. Damn it, they don't have to come after us; we're not important. We're nobodies, Irma. All we are to them is sport.' He shrugged again. 'If Newman and company want to play, I aim to oblige them! They're out to get us and I aim to get them first.' The more so now he knew about old Thad's private collection.

'But, Tom, how do you imagine you're going to get them?'

'I've worked out a plan.'

'You're deluding yourself, Tom.'

He shook his head. 'No. I'm happy. And I ain't having that happiness snatched away. I know what's got to be done and I aim to do it.'

★　★　★

Duffy watched as Thaddeus led his hunting party out of town, Red Antelope riding just a little behind him. Duffy guessed the scout would take the lead when the party was clear of town. Duffy spat; Easterners all he thought. Men who saw this expedition as nothing more than another hunting trip. It mattered little to them that the prey was two-legged.

'I believe you've hunted all over the world Mr Newman.' Matt Duke, who ran Garland's burgeoning newspaper ran beside Thaddeus.

'I have indeed.' Thaddeus was

235

inclined to be affable and laughed. 'There's not much about hunting big game anyone can teach me.'

'Good luck, Mr Newman,' Matt Duke replied.

Duffy thinned his lips. Duke knew damn well Newman was conducting a manhunt. What in tarnation was wrong with the man? Duffy took a deep breath and forced himself to relax. The next thing Duke would be writing was Newman's obituary. The railroad man had been trampling folk under foot for far too long. This time he was going to be stopped.

Duffy knew Cavendish was headed for San Paolo and could not think why. Duffy took a puff of his cigar. If Newman were fool enough to go after Cavendish then Cavendish intended to see Thaddeus and his hunting party dead. But why kick off from San Paolo?

★　★　★

The hardest part, Cavendish reflected, would be to leave Irma. She did not know that she was not riding with him. As they approached San Paolo Cavendish braced himself.

'It seems one time when Newman reckoned a certain *hombre* was sticking his nose into matters which did not concern him that *hombre* ended up minus his nose. The man's varmint through and through!'

'It ain't like you to run scared, Thomas.' Irma's brow furrowed. 'Where's this leading? If you're trying to tell me you're partial to your nose, well, I'm kinda partial to my own.'

'We ain't talking about noses, Irma.'

'Then what the hell are we talking about? You've a look on your face I don't much care for.'

Cavendish took a deep breath. 'The fact is, Irma, I've got to leave you in a place of safety. It's for your own good.'

'The hell it is!'

'I just can't have you along slowing me down. You just ain't got the stamina!

I'm coming back for you. Just as soon as I've dealt with Newman. My aunt will take good care of you. Pa's sister. I trust her just as much as I trust — '

'I ain't staying with your damn aunt, Thomas.'

Thomas Cavendish made no response. There was no arguing with a stubborn woman. But Irma had failed to realize that she wasn't being given a choice.

*   *   *

Red Antelope was forced to ride at the back of the column and eat dust. He kept his own counsel. And he kept his ears open. As far as these men were concerned he might as well not exist. After he had stated that Cavendish was headed for San Paolo he'd been ordered to drop back. And threatened should he be mistaken.

'If you let me down, I'll have your hide,' Newman had threatened.

Red Antelope believed he knew

Cavendish's intention. He would use the land to kill these men who pursued him. Red Antelope sensed that Cavendish was as one with the land.

'Remember,' Cavendish had said, before he had ridden away from Garland, 'Newman does not make idle threats. And I guess he ain't a jesting man. Keep your ears open, Scout, and your eyes peeled, and I ain't talking about earning your wage.' Cavendish had winked. 'Figure it out, if you're smart enough!'

'I'll have your hide,' Thaddeus Newman had said. The scout frowned, Cavendish knew something he did not.

★　★　★

The old man saw the lone rider; a man with two horses.

Cavendish cursed softly. He was displeased at being spotted, but there was nothing for it but to keep on. He reined to a halt before the oldster.

'If you're aiming to cross, best swing

west,' the oldster advised. 'That's where the water-holes lie.'

'Thanks for the advice, old-timer, but I know what I'm about,' Cavendish rejoined.

'I doubt it.' The oldster kept pace as Thomas moved on. 'I'll ride with you a way.'

'I wouldn't advise it. I've a hunting party on my tail,' Cavendish warned.

'You're an owlhoot then?' the oldster queried.

'If you're thinking of collecting a reward you can forget it, you old buzzard,' Cavendish advised. 'I ain't wanted, at least in the way you mean. And the fact is I'm a lawman myself.'

'So you say!'

'So I say. Now ride alongside me. I ain't fool enough to let you backshoot me.'

'That ain't my way, Lawman. I ain't never harmed no one who didn't deserve it.'

Cavendish dismounted, the sun hung like a hot ball in the sky. Methodically he began to unload the horses.

'Lord, you ain't crossing on foot?'

'Yep.'

'You're loco.'

'Not loco enough to ride where I'm headed. A burro maybe, but horses well . . . '

'You ain't having Betsy.'

'I don't want your damn burro, you old buzzard, but maybe others will. Get yourself out of here. I'm turning these horses free!'

'I don't want them. You can't beat a good burro.' The oldster placed a wad of tobacco between his gums. 'So you're taking the dead man's trail?'

'Yep,' Cavendish rejoined.

'Only one man made it across as far as I know,' the oldster observed.

'I've ridden the dead man's trail,' Cavendish smiled. 'Of course, at the time I didn't know it was the dead man's trail. Pa took me across. Wouldn't take Ivy though. Said it was no place for a woman. She wouldn't speak to either of us for a month.' He fell silent, Irma had threatened the cessation of conjugal rights.

'Hell's bells, now I know you. You're related to that crazy man Clem Cavendish.' The oldster scratched his head. 'You won't have to worry none about young Patrick Kaye. I've sent him on his way. Had him escorted to Mark Brain.'

Cavendish waited. There was more to come. 'Fact is, Kaye tried to kill me and steal my Betsy. Fact is, Kaye was wearing a mighty fancy type of ring.'

'A silver skull,' Cavendish mused. 'Kaye took it off a drifter he blasted. I was out of town at the time.'

The oldster cackled. 'Fact is, I reckon that ring belonged to Mark Brain's brother. Young Patrick Kaye is gonna end up in Brain's skillet. And he won't die easy . . . '

'You old buzzard, you could have put a bullet through his eyes.'

'I take my own vengeance; I don't rely on the Lord.'

'You sound like Thaddeus Newman.

And I reckon he's worse than Brain. Old Thad hunts for fun and mounts the skins, and I ain't talking about four-legged critters. Watch out for yourself and Betsy.'

The oldster chewed vigorously. 'Good luck. If you ever fall foul of Mark Brain just you tell him Old Cougar says to leave you be.'

Cavendish nodded. 'Thanks, old-timer. Have a care.' Cougar he reflected had turned into a mangy coyote but was still deadly as Patrick Kaye would doubtless discover. Cavendish's stomach churned. This was a merciless land and it bred a merciless kind of man.

'Say, Cavendish,' the oldster cackled, 'who the hell gave you that black eye? And the scratch? Don't tell me I know. Did I tell you I'm an admirer of Brigham Young?'

'I reckon he never got a black eye,' Cavendish observed, 'or he might have settled for just one woman.'

The oldster scratched his chin. 'I reckon not,' he observed solemnly.

Newman gazed up at the convent. It was situated on a small hill overlooking the hovels which called themselves a town.

'He's not that far ahead!' Newman's mouth was a grim line. 'And he'll be running scared. A scared man makes mistakes!'

'That's an odd choice for a convent!' Slim McCloud pointed upwards at the black stone walls.

Newman shrugged. 'They never venture out, I've heard. All transactions are carried out through a grille at the gate. They're enclosed.' He grinned. 'Why, the last young romeo to climb over those walls looking for a good-looking young woman was thrown out looking like a mule had kicked him. Seems Mother Angelina is no angel. And it wasn't worth the risk. They're all as ugly as sin.'

Everyone laughed at the joke.

Newman led the way forward towards

the small town of San Paolo. Behind him, the comments concerning the enclosed sisters became ribald.

'Goddamnit it, Sister Cavendish, I want out of here,' Irma raged.

Clem Cavendish's sister gave her a kindly smile. 'You're safe enough here until Thomas gets back. Besides, if you leave he won't know where to find you and you'll never be able to find him.'

'If he gets back!'

'It can be done. My brother . . . ' She sighed. 'Let's say he had his failings but lying was not one of them. His yarns sounded wild but they were certainly true.'

Irma snorted.

'There's plenty for you to read,' Sister Angelina continued. 'Novelettes concerning affairs of the heart.'

'Here? In this place?'

'A well-wisher sends them. And I haven't the heart to refuse them. Young

Amanda Brain. When she's finished with them she has her husband drop by with a boxful.'

'Not Mark Brain!' Irma had heard about Mark Brain.

'Naturally they are passed to us through the grille. And I must say they are well received . . . '

Irma sat down. 'I'm beaten. I feel as though I'm going mad. And I think your whole family must be mad!'

'Which only goes to show Thomas was right to leave you. It's clear you're in need of rest, sound sleep and good food, all of which you will find here.'

'Not to mention the novelettes! Good Lord, Cavendish was penning one himself. You don't pass them on to Ivy Tucker, do you, Sister?'

Sister Cavendish smiled. 'Naturally we don't mention our recipients.'

★   ★   ★

Thomas Cavendish gazed downwards. He'd made it. He was at the rim. His body was drenched with sweat and his heart was racing. Purposely he'd left a boot halfway up the climb. The old coot was still watching him. Removing his hat, Cavendish waved. Down below the old man did likewise. Replacing his hat, Cavendish set his mind to the task ahead.

★ ★ ★

Patrick Kaye was finally face to face with Mark Brain. He was not the monster he had been expecting. Brain possessed a pleasant-featured, roundish face, a beaming moon-shaped face which suggested simplicity of mind.

To Patrick's mind, Brain sounded like a simpleton, repeatedly asking how Betsy was keeping.

'I've a deal I want to put to you,' Patrick said, his confidence returning by the minute.

The men who had escorted him to Brain's ramshackle hideaway had kept quiet about the state they'd found him in. And, as far as Patrick knew, none of them was aware he'd wanted to blast the old buzzard and make off with the burro.

'You tell me over food,' Brain replied. 'Chicken,' he added.

The thought of eating with Brain made Patrick feel queasy, but seeing as it was chicken he could hardly refuse. A noise from his stomach reminded him he was hungry. And he must humour this monster. The thought of Thomas Cavendish disappearing, piece by piece, down this man's throat certainly appealed to Patrick. If Brain was as bad as gossip had it then he was just the man Patrick needed.

The chicken was well cooked and tasted good. Patrick sank his teeth into a chicken leg, but instead of tearing flesh kept his teeth clamped, suddenly aware that Brain was regarding him in a most odd fashion.

'That's a peculiar-looking ring. Mind if I take a closer look?' Brain's voice was mild.

'Keep it.' Patrick removed the ring, certain that Brain was angling for a gift.

'Where'd you get it?' Brain winked. 'You can tell me. There ain't no secrets between friends.'

Patrick hesitated. Silence ensued and then one of the gang began to relate a bloodthirsty yarn.

'There ain't a word of truth in what he's said,' Brain laughed. 'Your turn now, Pat.'

Patrick Kaye found himself embellishing the tale of the drifter's death. He turned the hapless stranger into a gunman of some repute. A man who could have taken McGinley himself.

'You're a damn liar,' someone said.

Patrick laughed. But his laughter soon died, No one else was laughing and Mark Brain's expression was changing. Colour darkened his skin and his eyes became malevolent.

With a violent motion, Brain swept his plate of chicken to the floor where it was eagerly pounced upon by one of the dogs found within the ramshackle camp. 'I've lost my taste for chicken,' Brain hollered. 'I fancy something different!'

Before he could even think, Patrick Kaye found himself grabbed from behind. Before his horrified gaze. Brain drew a wicked-looking knife. Patrick Kaye threshed desperately. No one paid him any attention. Brain's assorted crew continued to shovel chicken as though their lives depended upon it.

'I guess I'll have to eat alone!' Mark Brain smacked his lips, and then wiped a tear from his eye. 'That was my brother you killed.'

Patrick Kaye screamed. That old bastard had known what he was doing. He had spotted the ring. He'd known all along.

Brain grinned. 'Goddamn it he's fainted clean away. But I'm a patient *hombre*. I can wait until he comes round. Meanwhile, one of you men get my slicing knives!'

12

'Such a short man,' the woman giggled. 'And his woman was so tall and so angry. Why, she would not speak to him, and he had a black eye!' There was a hint of admiration in the floosie's voice.

Berresford, the banker, swore. He was truly shocked. Cavendish's worth as a man plummeted in his estimation. What kind of man was the ex-sheriff of Salt Creek that he'd let a woman punch him in the eye?

'And the sisters they are so ugly they are afraid to be seen,' the woman continued. 'Why else do they never leave their prison?'

'How was Cavendish when he left town?' Newman demanded. He slapped a coin on the bar. 'How was his manner? Did he seem afraid? Was he angry?'

The woman shrugged. 'He was whistling, senor,' she replied simply.

'Whistling!' Berresford stated in amazement. He felt a frisson of unease which he quickly dismissed as non-sense. Cavendish did not sound like a man who knew death followed him. Cavendish was not behaving as a frightened man on the run should behave.

No one bothered to ask Red Antelope's opinion. Only a fool would allow a woman to slow him down whilst he raced for his life. If anything, Cavendish was a shrewd man who had calculated the risks. The scout smiled slightly. Had anyone asked him he could have told them where the woman was to be found. What better place was there in which to hide a woman than within a house of women? A place into which men did not venture.

'Find me that renegade lawman, Indian!' Newman bellowed, suddenly rounding on the tracker.

'I will find him.' Red Antelope

understood why Cavendish's eye had been blacked. Probably Cavendish would have forced her inside, the woman screeching she did not wish to remain behind.

'I've a hunch,' Berresford murmured, 'that this time it won't be so easy!'

Newman snorted. 'Good. You men need a challenge. But I cannot honestly see Cavendish as a worthy opponent.'

Red Antelope thought differently: he knew where Cavendish was going. Cavendish rode the dead man's trail, so called because the unfortunates who had taken that particular route seldom made it across.

Cavendish, Red Antelope decided, was a good judge of men. The lawman had known that the scout would not be fooled. He had also known that Red Antelope disdained to hunt women considering them unworthy of a warrior's skill. Without a word, glancing neither to left nor right Red Antelope led the hunting party past the low hill upon which the convent stood. There were no signs of life, no signs that women lived behind the towering thick stone walls and heavy wooden door.

★ ★ ★

The old man watched from a distance as the Indian tracker led the hunting party to the place where Thomas Cavendish had made his ascent.

'Damn fools,' the oldster muttered as one of the fancy dudes, gesticulating excitedly, pointed out Cavendish's discarded boot.

Ignoring the scout, the hunting party surged forward and upwards. The oldster's breath whistled through his teeth. He knew what was going to happen. And it did.

As shale began to slide from beneath its rear hooves, the last horse in the convoy lost its footing. Snorting with terror, it began to slide backwards. Going down on the slide it crushed its rider beneath its flank. Screams of pain and curses broke the awesome silence of the desert.

It did not occur to Newman that Cavendish was endeavouring to lead them to their death. To Thaddeus, Slim's accident was an unfortunate mishap. It also served to delay the party.

'He's hurt! Badly!' Berresford, who had descended, hollered. 'His ribs are stove in and the horse is a gonna!'

'He'll die before we can find medical help,' a companion stated the obvious.

'I wouldn't let an animal suffer the way Slim is suffering.' Thaddeus's voice quivered with false emotion.

His companions murmured words of similar fashion. Everyone remembered the pact they always made before setting out to hunt game.

'Then we're agreed,' Thaddeus's voice was now brisk and business-like.

There were murmurs of agreement.

'For the Lord's sake, help me,' Slim screamed. 'You can't do this, Thaddeus. You can't!'

Berresford, they all observed, had

stepped out of the line of fire. Helplessly, Slim stared upwards at his companions. Thaddeus sighted his rifle. A shot rang out. Slim's body jerked: he was out of his misery. Thaddeus then shot the horse.

'What damn fools,' the old man muttered. Surely they could see that Cavendish had deliberately chosen this route across the Badlands, a route no sane man travelled?

Eyes squinting, the old man watched as a heated discussion ensued. Some, it seemed, wanted to bury the body, but the big man who led the hunting party prevailed. Leaving their companion where he lay the others resumed the hunt.

Judging the time right, the old man approached. The man who had been shot was a young man, too young to be hunting someone such as Cavendish. The oldster took the rifle, rummaged through the dead man's pockets, taking what he found, and then turned his attention to the clothes and boots.

Afterwards, as always, he took care to obliterate his tracks. The horse would provide dried meat, although it would be some task taking what he needed. Already the first buzzard had landed.

The oldster cackled. Cavendish one less to worry about!

Red Antelope's admiration for Cavendish grew. He knew the thoughts of the man they hunted. Deliberately, he had chosen the path no man wanting to live would tread.

Red Antelope had felt eyes watching them. The old man, he who scavenged upon the men who tried to cross over and failed, was watching. Red Antelope knew him. From time to time their paths had crossed.

A sombre atmosphere prevailed that night, the men remembering their fallen companion. Although none had spoken against the deed, Thaddeus could feel the unspoken condemnation. Unknowingly he made a fatal error of judgement.

'I've been saving this to celebrate

Cavendish's capture. And the girl,' he added as an afterthought. Along the way hanging the woman had become immaterial, Cavendish had become his adversary.

Whistles of appreciation broke out when the group saw the bottles of wine Thaddeus produced. The age of the wine was lost upon Red Antelope. Silently he slipped away into the darkness. Squatting down he observed the party.

Tomorrow would be worse than today. Cavendish was leading them into a maze of narrow passageways which would force them to ride in single file and to double back upon themselves many times. And the water-holes which lay ahead would be poisoned.

Drawing his knife, Red Antelope hacked at a cactus plant he carried at his belt. He sucked the pulp chewing on the fleshy part of the plant.

Cavendish had no need to kill these men, the land would do it for him.

Voices grew loud. Men reminisced

about old times. In the flickering light thrown out by the camp-fire, Red Antelope watched as a book was passed from hand to hand. Finally the camp slept.

Red Antelope returned to camp as dawn broke. The book lay where it had been placed. Red Antelope, crouching beside the spent embers of the fire, turned the pages of this very important book. The muscles of his jaw twitched.

'Where the hell have you been?' Newman roared. Coming awake he saw the scout crouched over the fire. The smell of coffee and cooking biscuits pervaded the air. Newman did not expect an answer.

★　★　★

The hunted man led the way through twisting passageways eating into and through the rocks which barred his path. The passageways were not places for horses. Anyone coming through would be forced to ride single file. The way was seemingly endless. Cavendish whistled cheerfully.

Of them all, Red Antelope would know the danger, but the Indian scout was being paid to track not to voice any kind of opinion. Red Antelope pointed. He did not bother to point out that the man they hunted was now on foot.

'How far ahead?' Newman demanded.

'He is near,' Red Antelope replied. 'Where he leads, I will follow.'

'He's led us into a maze,' Turner grumbled. Back home, he was a successful man: he had a wife and three marriageable daughters. Turner had jumped at the chance of joining the manhunt.

'Life's just too damn boring.' He'd been relaxing at his club, cigar in his hand and a glass of fine whiskey before him upon the mahogany table.

'And he knows this land,' Berresford stated. The lawman knew exactly where he was going.

'We're not going home with our tails

between our legs,' Newman snarled. 'We're going to get the bastard. And you're correct, Berresford. This is going to be the hardest of them all. I'll admit it, I underestimated the man.'

'So you'll take your hat off to him and then skin him!' Berresford jested.

'You know me!' Thaddeus replied.

It was then Crowhurst's animal went down, its forefoot going into a narrow crevice. Crowhurst's leg was squashed against the hard, jagged, rock wall of the passageway. He screamed with pain.

Some distance away, Cavendish heard the sound of a shot closely followed by a second shot. Cavendish halted a moment trying to put himself in Newman's boots. He guessed Newman would decline to tote along injured companions. He also guessed that come what may, Newman would not turn around and head home as a sane *hombre* might be expected to do.

'My God!' Turner yelled. 'He must have poisoned the waterhole. The bastard has poisoned the water.'

And so he had, Thaddeus Newman reflected. And even put up a warning of sorts: a crudely drawn skull and crossbones scratched out in red chalk upon a nearby rock.

★ ★ ★

Cavendish made camp. Long before they got through the Badlands, Newman's party would run out of water. Cavendish shook his head. He was weary of the whole business. He wanted it over. In the darkness, a short distance from his bedroll, a skull gleamed white.

During the night Red Antelope slipped away. He went on foot having been ordered to give his horse to Crowhurst.

'I'll have that red devil's hide,' Newman blustered. They could not go back, Newman realized that now. Cavendish had led them into a maze. Deliberately so. Without the scout they would have a hell of a task retracing their footsteps. Also, to be beaten by an insignificant bum such as Cavendish would wipe out the respect he commanded. Men would die if they went back, and they would die if they went forward, for Cavendish would have ensured there would not be water ahead.

'We go on,' Newman answered the unspoken question.

'I'm going back.' Berresford's nerve broke.

'Good luck to you then.' Newman knew when to be magnanimous. 'But you'll miss one hell of a party when I catch up with Cavendish . . . '

'Me, too. I'm sorry.' Crowhurst could not meet Newman's eyes.

Newman led the men who remained with him onwards. Something bothered him, but he could not think what it might be. The sun was beginning to climb in the sky before Newman worked out what it was. His sketchbook had been put back inside its carrier. Stopping, Newman thrust a hand into the leather satchel. He pulled out his book. Newman's exhibits were mounted in glass cabinets and he'd sketched his trophies just as they stood. He was pretty sure he had not returned the sketchbook, and the scout . . .

Newman shook his head and tried to dismiss his unease.

Cavendish began his day filled with optimism; Newman began his day with a howl of anger followed by a string of threats. Four objects lay placed near his sleeping place: four charred objects which had once been feet.

'Why?' Granger exclaimed. 'For the Lord's sake, tell me why?'

'That's why.' Newman opened his book. He flicked through until he found the sketch of an Indian chief complete with war bonnet and tomahawk.

Granger was sick. 'Berresford,' he murmured. 'Crowhurst.'

'Pull yourself together, man,' Newman snarled. 'He won't have gone away. We might be dogging Cavendish but now we've got that varmint dogging us.'

Granger, to Newman's disgust, began to cry.

★ ★ ★

Cavendish did not fear snakes; he found them fascinating. Clem Cavendish had not killed snakes when Tom had been around for Tom's rage, small though he had been, had about matched Clem's own.

A large rattlesnake slid across the toe of Tom's boot. He watched its progress. He was quite at ease. He'd been right to leave Irma. She would not have been at ease here. Snakes basked on the rocks or slithered across the passageway. There was a surfeit of them here, not being so easy for them to leave. Last thing he'd want was to have Miz Irma screeching in horror at the sight of the basking reptiles. Moving very carefully, Cavendish set his foot down upon the next large flat stone. Many years back Clem had traversed this passageway. Oddly enough, Clem had admitted to being in mortal terror. Thomas felt perfectly safe here. Safer than he had done whilst in Salt Creek.

He wondered which one his sister would choose. McGinley or Moss. Neither he reckoned. Maybe she'd settle for both of them. Ivy Tucker wasn't about to say 'I do' for the second time. And Cissie would go East and be a lady. Cavendish frowned; unless Newman was permanently dealt with, he wouldn't dare send his sister a missive. A polecat such as Newman would be sure to bribe the post office clerk. Cavendish gritted his teeth. That woman wouldn't need bribing, she was a friend of Mrs Pole.

Newman struggled on. They were on foot now. And only three remained, himself and his two companions. They were making slow progress. As gentlemen they were accustomed to better conditions. Thaddeus's boots had blistered his heel. Every step was pain. And with each step his hatred of Cavendish grew. He had not known it was possible to hate a man he had never seen with such vehemence. An insignificant little man who . . .

'This way!' McBain pointed. Cavendish had dropped a handkerchief.

'No! He wants us to follow.' Granger had had enough.

'Damnit man, you can't go back. You'll die.'

'We'll die if we go on.' Granger shook his head. 'I think we can certainly expect Sheriff Cavendish to have laid on another surprise.'

'Do you want to end up like Berresford?' Newman snarled. 'You don't have an inkling, do you, Granger, what that devil might have done to them before crisping their feet. Let me spell it out . . . '

'I'm with Newman.' McBain's face had blanched.

Granger sobbed as the other two entered the passageway. His will to survive broken, he sat down and buried his head in his hands. He did not have long to wait before he heard the first yell of terror, the voice he recognized as belonging to McBain.

They didn't see them at first, although the reptiles were not hidden. It was McBain who stepped upon the first basking snake. Rattling, it struck, and McBain in his terror grabbed at Thaddeus and managed to take him down with him. Raising his head, Thaddeus stared into the eyes of the largest rattler he had ever seen. There it was before his eyes, ready to strike.

And then, from nowhere an arrow struck the snake pinning its head to the ground as the scaled body threshed as it died.

★   ★   ★

'Well that learned him,' Mark Brain said to no one in particular. Throughout the day he had made the same observation at least a dozen times. He tossed the bone to the ground where it was eagerly fallen upon by the dogs which lived around the perimeter of Brain's camp.

★ ★ ★

Thaddeus Newman walked out of Death Canyon. No longer upright and vigorous, Newman was a man who had been brought to his knees. Weakened by thirst he had still managed to get to his feet and carefully walk out. It was as though he had been walking on eggshells. Of Red Antelope, who had saved him, there was no sign. Newman staggered on, cursing the name of Cavendish.

Red Antelope easily overpowered Granger. He left the man tied and helpless. Grimly he set off in pursuit of Newman. Overtaking his quarry in the nick of time, he fitted an arrow to his bow and, without hesitation, saved Newman's life. And then, drawing back amongst the rocks, he watched as Newman made his way to safety.

Without fear, Red Antelope passed

269

through the canyon of death. He found Newman some distance away, spent and helpless, as he lay too exhausted to move, racked by the agony of thirst and barely conscious.

Newman gulped greedily as the canteen was placed to his parched lips. Tepid water trickled down his throat. Opening his eyes, Newman expected to see the mocking face of his hitherto unseen enemy Cavendish. Instead, as his vision cleared, he saw the familiar features of the scout Red Antelope.

'Many times,' Red Antelope said, 'have I wondered what fate befell my brother.'

Granger lay where he'd been left. Muted but distinguishable, Granger heard the screams of agony. They went on for a very long time before silence fell. Even then Granger writhed desperately, for he knew the fate in store for him.

★ ★ ★

Red Antelope looked down at what had been Thaddeus Newman. He laughed, and then he remembered Granger.

* * *

Thomas walked into Mexico. Choosing a spot, he set up an ambush. He was leaving nothing to chance. If any of the pursuers made it across they would die here. Cavendish chewed on a strip of dried meat and took a mouthful of tepid water. By and by, when he was sure it was safe, he'd go back for Irma. By a different route. And on horseback. Time dragged on; Cavendish grew stiff and weary and yet still he waited although in his heart he believed them dead.

And then he saw the lone figure travelling on foot just as he had travelled.

Red Antelope waved. After some time, Cavendish, moving cautiously, appeared.

'I have kept my word,' Red Antelope

said. 'I have tracked you down.'

'And!'

'And go back to your woman.' Red Antelope moved onwards heading into Mexico.

Cavendish did not ask what had happened to the hunting party. That was not his concern. It was enough to know he would not be seeing any of them.

Maybe he'd be bringing misfortune upon himself by getting hitched to Irma. Maybe he'd best reconsider. However, he'd see her northwards, take her to safety as he'd promised.

Cavendish grinned. And along the way unashamedly take advantage of Irma's gratitude. Naturally enough her gratitude was bound to wear thin, but while it lasted it would be something.

Which meant he'd best get back to the convent with all possible speed. Irma was wild enough to take off without him and he was damned if he was going to miss out on all that was due to come his way. Having already sampled Irma's gratitude he knew damn well what was in store for him and it was more than worth a black eye.

'Hold up, Red Antelope,' he hollered.

The scout turned.

'Can you find me a horse pretty damn quick?'

The scout nodded.

'Then lead on. I aim to take your advice.'

Whistling cheerfully, Thomas Cavendish followed in the footsteps of Red Antelope.

THE END

We do hope that you have enjoyed reading this large print book.

Did you know that all of our titles are available for purchase?

We publish a wide range of high quality large print books including:
Romances, Mysteries, Classics
General Fiction
Non Fiction and Westerns

Special interest titles available in large print are:
The Little Oxford Dictionary
Music Book, Song Book
Hymn Book, Service Book

Also available from us courtesy of Oxford University Press:
Young Readers' Dictionary
(large print edition)
Young Readers' Thesaurus
(large print edition)

For further information or a free brochure, please contact us at:
Ulverscroft Large Print Books Ltd.,
The Green, Bradgate Road, Anstey,
Leicester, LE7 7FU, England.
Tel: (00 44) **0116 236 4325**
Fax: (00 44) **0116 234 0205**